## Date Due

| | | | | | |
|---|---|---|---|---|---|
| | | | | | |
| | | | | | |
| | | | | | |
| | | | | | |
| | | | | | |
| | | | | | |
| | | | | | |
| | | | | | |
| | | | | | |

# ASTEROIDS

## INVADERS FROM SPACE

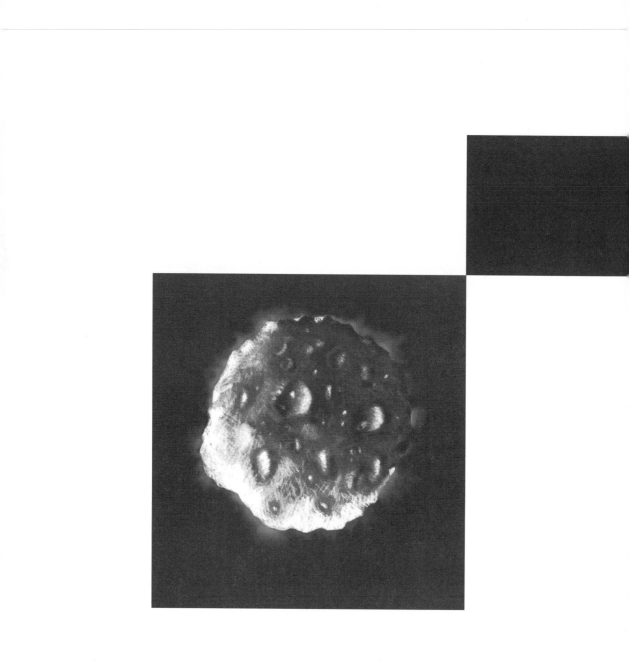

ATHENEUM BOOKS FOR YOUNG READERS

# ASTEROIDS

## INVADERS FROM SPACE

BY
**ROBERT KRASKE**

Illustrated with Photographs
and with Maps and Drawings
by the Author

# For Steven, Philip, and Lisa

Atheneum Books for Young Readers
An imprint of Simon & Schuster Children's Publishing Division
1230 Avenue of the Americas
New York, New York 10020

Book design by PIXEL PRESS

The text of this book is set in Bodoni Book

First edition
Printed in the United States of America

10  9  8  7  6  5  4  3  2  1

Library of Congress Cataloging-in-Publication Data
Kraske, Robert.
Asteroids: invaders from space / by Robert Kraske: illustrated
with photographs and with maps and drawings by author.
p. cm.
Includes bibliographical references and index.
Summary: Zooming in from space, asteroids have struck earth in the past
and will do so again in the future. How astronomers search near space for
these "flying rocks" and devise ways to avoid an impact that, in a
worst-case scenario, could eliminate civilization. Included: stories of
asteroids that have collided with earth; " Your Own Space Rock"
—collecting meteorites (fragments of larger asteroids).

ISBN 0-689-31860-X
1. Asteroids—Juvenile literature. [1. Asteroids.] I. Title.
QB651.K69   1995   94-8072
523.4'4—dc20

# Contents

# Acknowledgments

Many people contributed to the preparation of this book—astronomers, earth scientists, librarians, photo researchers, and more.

Especially helpful were Margaret A. Huss, American Meteorite Laboratory, Denver, Colorado, and Gary Huss, Ph.D., California Institute of Technology, Division of Geology and Planetary Sciences, Pasadena, who reviewed the supplement titled "Your Own Space Rock."

Eleanor Helin, Ph.D., California Institute of Technology, Jet Propulsion Laboratory, Pasadena, read the manuscript. Dr. Helin is an astronomer and a pioneer in near-earth asteroid research. She is among a small group of space and earth scientists engaged in expanding our knowledge of these cosmic rocks booming along through dark and cold space, where our fragile blue planet is a fellow voyager. Her comments did much to clarify a constantly evolving subject.

## TARGET EARTH IN SPACE

For more than 4 billion years, Earth has circled
the sun amid swarms of asteroids and comets.
In the past, some of these flying space objects
have slammed into our planet and will do so
again in the future. Our view of target Earth is
from a point above the moon's surface. Two
hundred forty thousand miles away in space,
night advances across Africa.
NASA

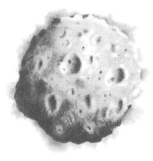

"**D**anger! Flying rocks!"

Space travelers passing Mars and heading for Jupiter might see this warning sign on a chart of the solar system, the sun's family of nine planets, including Earth.

The sign would point out the asteroid belt, a 100-million-mile-wide band of stones and rocks floating in high-speed orbit around the sun. The stones and rocks are called asteroids, tiny planets.

There are tens of thousands of flying rocks—too many to count. Yet astronomers today know that, despite the number of asteroids, the asteroid belt is mostly empty space. You could be in the very middle of the asteroid belt and not see a single one!

Our space travelers make a decision. They decide to delay their journey to Jupiter and take a sight-seeing tour of the asteroid belt, seek out the asteroids, cruise in and around and between them.

Millions of miles often separate asteroids in their flight around the sun. In the deep freeze of space, the side of an asteroid facing the sun never warms to more than -100° F.

In the pale light of the faraway sun, most of the asteroids appear small, some no larger than pebbles or golf balls. Others are boulders, bulky as a compact car. Still others match the height of a one-hundred-story office building. A few as large as Switzerland or Maine lumber by. And then something astonishing, the largest asteroid of all, a black monster the size of Montana, slowly rotating. Sunlight advances across bumpy flatlands, slides in and out of craters. An awesome sight.

The travelers note that the big asteroids tend to be round, but the smaller ones have odd shapes. Some resemble watermelons, bowling pins, fat cigars, even dumbbells. Pits and scars mar their dark surfaces, like those of peanut shells or lumpy potatoes.

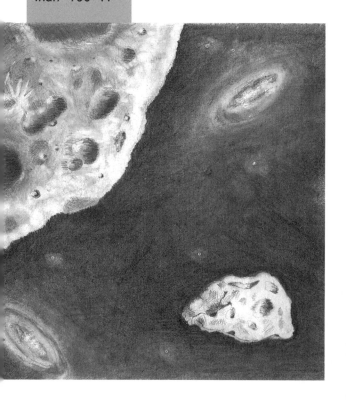

Then the travelers see a rare sight. Two asteroids the size of pianos collide, then bound apart. Fragments from the collision scatter and join other asteroids in their steady course around the sun.

But a chunk large as a loaf of bread breaks away, starts on a new path away from the band of asteroids. It heads for the sun, which seems the size of a ten-cent piece from out here, 300 million miles away through cold, dark space.

On its long solo flight toward that distant bright star, the rock will pass the orbits of Mars, Earth, Venus, and

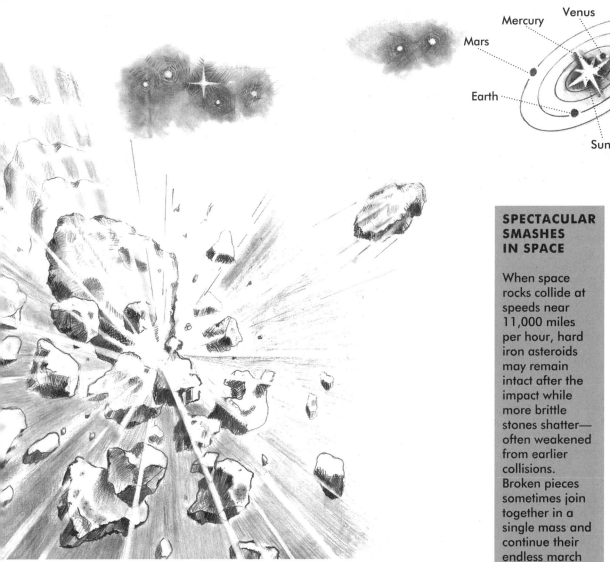

Mercury. If the speeding rock passes close to one of these planets, that planet's gravity will reel it in, and it will crash to the surface.

If Earth is that planet, people here may see the broken fragment, a fireball speeding along at ten miles per second, trailing smoke, and hear it rumbling like a freight train. At night, it could appear as a shooting star streaking across the night sky.

Here are four stories astronomers tell about asteroids that left the asteroid belt and found their way to earth. Three actually happened.

**SPECTACULAR SMASHES IN SPACE**

When space rocks collide at speeds near 11,000 miles per hour, hard iron asteroids may remain intact after the impact while more brittle stones shatter—often weakened from earlier collisions. Broken pieces sometimes join together in a single mass and continue their endless march in the asteroid belt. Other fragments might be ejected from the asteroid belt into deep space or toward the sun and the planets of the inner solar system.

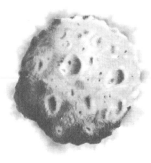

**A** day in eastern Arizona 50,000 years ago. Antelope and hairy elephants with curved tusks graze on the plain. Saber-toothed tigers watch, ready to charge. People do not as yet live in the region.

In the sky to the north, a fireball appears. Quickly it grows brighter than the sun. Alarmed, animals raise their heads.

Approaching earth at 43,000 miles per hour, the 150-foot-wide rock weighs perhaps 300,000 tons, as much as four aircraft carriers. It rams into the earth, punching a crater more than 700 feet deep and 4,100 feet wide, and instantly vaporizes in a blinding flash brighter than the sun.

The impact is about the same as 20 million tons of TNT—1,000 atom bombs. The blast sends 300 million tons of earth erupting into the sky. Rock and soil scatter for hundreds of miles. Dust hides the sun. A rim of ejected dirt 150 feet high is left around the crater.

Today, we call the hole made by the fireball Meteor Crater. Five miles south of Interstate 40, twenty miles west of Winslow, Arizona, the crater is the largest known asteroid impact in the U.S.

The space rock that made the crater had been nudged out of the asteroid belt, perhaps after rebounding from a collision with a larger asteroid. It may have orbited the sun for thousands of years. For all those years, its orbit crossed that of Earth's.

On a day 500 centuries ago, its course through space and Earth's course came together at the same moment and the two collided.

On that morning of June 30, 1908, one man saw the fireball streak across the sky, "so bright, even the light of the

Fifty thousand years ago, a nickel-iron meteorite nearly half the size of a football field slammed into earth at twelve miles per second, ten times faster than a rifle bullet, and blasted out Meteor Crater near Winslow, Arizona. Since the impact, the crater has filled in, but today it is still deep enough to hold a building fifty-five stories tall.
U.S. Geological Survey/ D. J. Roddy

sun appeared dark," he said later. The explosion followed. A glowing mushroom-shaped cloud appeared high above the forest near the Tunguska River in Siberia.

So powerful was the blast that people 600 miles distant heard it. Reindeer thirty miles away toppled over dead. Residents of Vanavara, fifty miles from the explosion, felt the heat and saw their windows crack and shatter. Ten miles farther on, the blast wave blew down tents of wandering sheepherders.

As the force of the explosion passed through the earth, instruments that measure earthquakes scrawled jiggly lines in London, England, 3,800 miles to the west.

That night and for several nights afterward, the sky over Europe glowed. People in Paris and London read newspapers outside at midnight.

But there was something strange about the explosion. The stupendous blast, as powerful as ten hydrogen bombs, left no crater. Investigators saw only what happened on the ground below the blast—trees bent, snapped, scorched, and flattened. The downed trees formed a circle for twenty-five miles in all directions, an area larger than Rhode Island.

For years, newspapers speculated about the cause of the mysterious event. The most popular explanation: A nuclear-powered spaceship carrying aliens from a distant planet had exploded as it was preparing to land.

Scientists studying the blast, however, came up with a more practical explanation. The blast, they said, was caused by the burned-out core of a dead comet as it entered the air blanket around Earth.

This explanation was accepted until early 1993. Then new studies showed that small comets exploded too high in the atmosphere to damage the ground below. The cause of the Tunguska blast was something else: an asteroid—or a fragment of a large asteroid—speeding into Earth's atmosphere at nearly 50,000 miles per hour and exploding

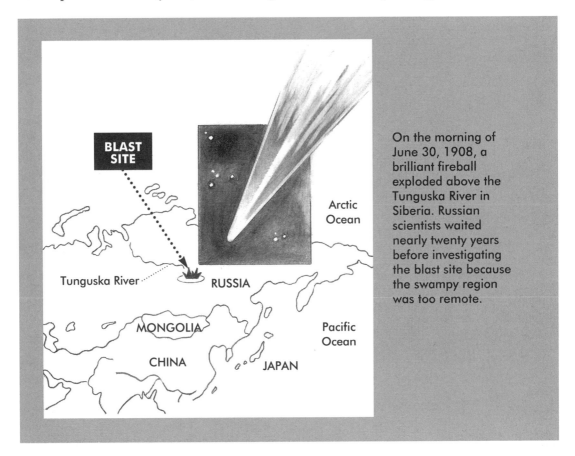

On the morning of June 30, 1908, a brilliant fireball exploded above the Tunguska River in Siberia. Russian scientists waited nearly twenty years before investigating the blast site because the swampy region was too remote.

six miles above the forest. Investigators, however, differed about the size of the object. Some said 100 feet wide, others 260 feet.

The nightly glow in the sky? Probably the result of the fireball of heated air carrying moisture into the upper atmosphere. The moisture froze and formed clouds. High-altitude winds transported the clouds across Europe. Sunlight reflecting off the clouds lighted the streets below after sunset.

The mystery of what caused the mysterious blast took eighty-five years to solve. Scientists were also left with a sobering thought. It was sheer luck that the rogue asteroid had detonated over an uninhabited, swampy forest. Had it appeared over Moscow just 2,300 miles to the west, tens of thousands of lives in Russia's capital city would have been instantly wiped out.

March 23, 1989, was a night much like any other. But while people on Earth watched TV, did homework, or slept, something unusual was going on in the night sky: A mighty asteroid was hurtling past Earth at 46,000 miles per hour.

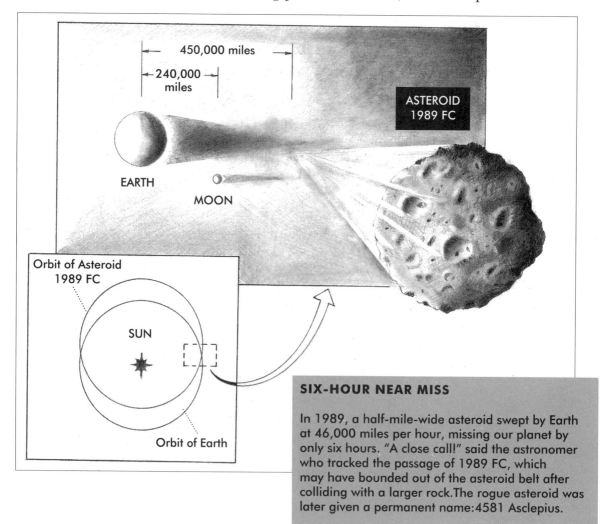

450,000 miles

240,000 miles

ASTEROID 1989 FC

EARTH

MOON

Orbit of Asteroid 1989 FC

SUN

Orbit of Earth

**SIX-HOUR NEAR MISS**

In 1989, a half-mile-wide asteroid swept by Earth at 46,000 miles per hour, missing our planet by only six hours. "A close call!" said the astronomer who tracked the passage of 1989 FC, which may have bounded out of the asteroid belt after colliding with a larger rock. The rogue asteroid was later given a permanent name: 4581 Asclepius.

Astronomers were astonished. They hadn't seen the asteroid approach—it came from the direction of the sun. At night, a full moon hid its glowing path among the stars. The asteroid, a half-mile-wide mountain of rock, passed within 450,000 miles of earth, less than twice as far away as the moon. It had missed crashing into Earth by only six hours.

"That was a close call," said Henry Holt, the observer from the University of Arizona who spotted the asteroid. A temporary identifying number, 1989 FC, was applied to his discovery. Later, it was permanently labeled 4581 Asclepius.

Such a near miss had not happened since 1937. Then, an asteroid called Hermes cruised by Earth at about the same distance. Astronomers call these close flybys "earth-grazers."

A collision between Earth and an earth-grazer the size of 4581 Asclepius would be catastrophic—a sudden, widespread disaster.

Scientists estimated that, if 4581 Asclepius had struck the earth, it could have punched a crater a mile deep and five to ten miles wide. Flaming rock bursting out of the crater would have fallen on homes and buildings fifty to ninety miles from the impact, destroying everything, including all people.

Crashing into the ocean, 4581 Asclepius would have created waves hundreds of feet high. Rushing toward land, the powerful waves would have swept over cities along the coast. If the object had struck the moon, rocks and dirt would have showered through space onto Earth.

An astronomer calculated the big rock's orbit around the sun at 380 days compared with Earth's 365 days. The next flyby of 4581 Asclepius took place in April 1990, when it passed earth at a distance of a few million miles, close enough to see with a handheld telescope.

That was the good news. More calculations showed that future orbits of 4581 Asclepius will bring it close to Earth again in the year 2015. "If our figures are correct," the astronomer noted, "the asteroid will have made twenty-five orbits around the sun to Earth's twenty-six, and we will meet again."

Astronomers could do nothing but report the bad news. An asteroid six miles wide was on a collision course with earth. It would strike within twenty-four hours. They hadn't spotted it before because, heading directly for Earth, it had appeared in the heavens as only another point of light.

The asteroid was traveling faster than a rifle bullet. Once it reached the air blanket around earth, it would begin to glow brighter than the sun. But by then it would be too late. People would have twenty seconds to take cover.

In the White House, the president read the astronomers' report. The asteroid would blast a crater 120 miles wide, an area as large as Maryland or Belgium. Air for thousands of miles would heat to 2,000 to 3,000°F. White-hot rock flung high into the sky and carried around the globe by swift winds would set entire cities and forests on fire. Two-thirds of all people on Earth would perish. Survivors—people in far corners of the world—faced living on a ruined planet.

The president put down the report. He turned to his advisors.

"What should we do?"

There were no answers.

# 3 Target Earth

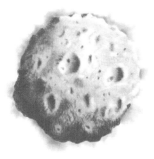

A six-mile-wide rock zooming in from space and slamming into earth is not a science fiction story. It has happened in the past and could happen again.

Earth exists in a cosmic shooting gallery. As our planet moves around the sun, it travels among a swarm of asteroids and comets. Some of these objects will, sooner or later, collide with our planet. Only recently have astronomers learned just how often asteroids, large and small, strike Earth.

Eugene Shoemaker, a former geologist with the U.S. Geological Survey in Flagstaff, Arizona, calculated how often big ones collide with Earth.

A comet or asteroid a half mile in diameter, he estimated, strikes Earth about once every 100,000 years. About five objects a mile or so in diameter collide with Earth every million years on average.

How many asteroids of this size are "out there"?

Astronomers and earth scientists now study past impacts of large asteroids on Earth. This is a painting of a superasteroid 500 miles in diameter that may have wiped out organisms living on our planet 3.5 billion years ago. The only survivors of the blast may have lived thousands of feet underwater. NASA

Eleanor Helin, an astronomer with the National Aeronautics and Space Administration, Jet Propulsion Laboratory, Asteroid Project, started the first search for near-Earth asteroids in the early 1970s. She answers the question this way:

"The best estimate is that there are 1,500 to 2,000 asteroids one-half mile in diameter or larger in near-Earth orbits. Under extreme conditions, these are all candidates for collision with earth."

"Near-Earth" means that the paths—or orbits—these asteroids take around the sun cross the orbit of earth. If Earth and an asteroid arrive at the same point in space at the same time, the gravity of the larger body, Earth, will pull in the smaller body and the two will collide.

The half-milers, though, are mere boulders compared with the big bruisers. These large asteroids, five to six miles wide, strike Earth every 100 million years.

"There is a possibility that a large asteroid could collide with Earth, destroying life as we know it," Helin says. "It has happened a number of times in the past. We know that events like this will occur in the future, but we don't know when. The objects are out there."

While such an event is sure to happen someday, the chance that a large Earth-crosser will collide with earth in any one year is slim indeed. Still, the possibility exists. Such an impact would be a disaster for our entire planet.

Evidence gathered in the last twenty years suggests that impacts by asteroids or comets have played a major role in the history of life on Earth. Most astronomers and earth scientists now believe that an asteroid six miles wide collided with Earth 65 million years ago. The blast created conditions that wiped out the dinosaurs and most of the other plants and animals on earth. It could happen again.

Are we doomed then? Are we helpless before the threat of a killer asteroid zooming in from space without warning and destroying our planet and civilization?

Preventing a large asteroid from hitting Earth may be possible, space scientists say. "We could probably do something to prevent the impact, given enough time," concludes Eleanor Helin. "But we must learn far in advance that the object's orbit is on a collision course with Earth."

## THE SOLAR SYSTEM: VAST, EMPTY SPACES

Distances in our solar system are difficult to grasp. How can we visualize the millions and billions of miles of empty space among planets? If we reduce the solar system to the size of a football field, however, the spaces become clearer. The sun, about the size of a six-inch grapefruit on the goal line, would be circled by Earth on the eighteen-yard line. Before colliding with Earth, an asteroid would have to travel the vast distance from the sixty-eighty yard lines.

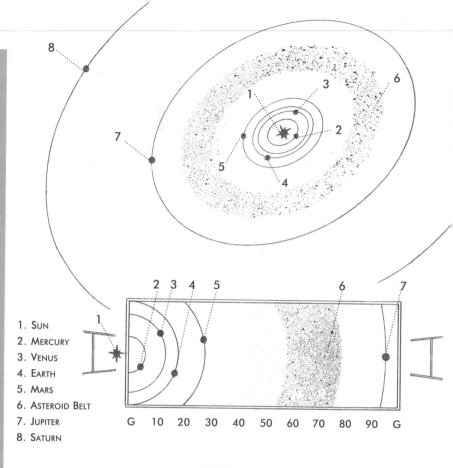

1. SUN
2. MERCURY
3. VENUS
4. EARTH
5. MARS
6. ASTEROID BELT
7. JUPITER
8. SATURN

G  10  20  30  40  50  60  70  80  90  G

## BLUE EARTH IN SPACE

In February 1990, from beyond Pluto, the outermost planet in the solar system, *Voyager 1* recorded Earth 3.7 billion miles away in empty space. The far-off blue dot—where dinosaurs once roamed, now home to 5.5 billion humans—suggests the enormous distances asteroids and comets travel to reach our tiny planet in the vastness of the solar system.
NASA/JPL

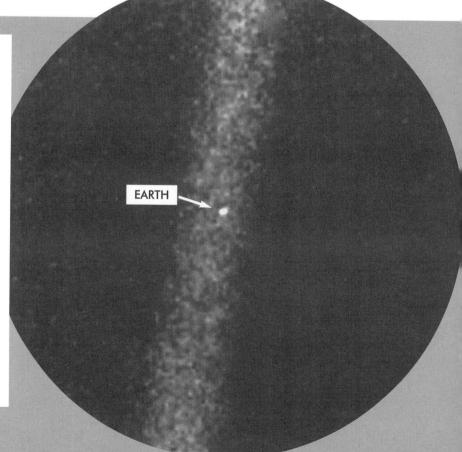

EARTH

# Playground of the Asteroids

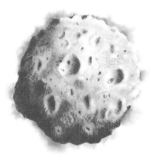

An asteroid, whether in the asteroid belt or cruising among the inner planets of the solar system, travels immense distances.

Its playing field is the solar system, our sun's family of nine planets—Mercury, Venus, Earth, Mars, Jupiter, Saturn, Uranus, Neptune, and Pluto. Our solar system is a small part of the Milky Way galaxy (or group of stars), which is, in turn, only one of 10 billion or so galaxies in the universe. So vast is the empty space between the sun and its family of planets and between the planets themselves that our minds reel trying to comprehend these distances.

In the solar system, Mercury is the closest planet to the sun, about 36 million miles away. Mercury takes 88 days to travel around the sun. Earth, the third planet from the sun, 93 million miles distant, requires 365 days. The outermost planet, 3,670 million miles from the sun, Pluto takes 248 years to make just one trip around our star. (Since it was discovered in 1930, Pluto has still to complete a single orbit.)

# THE SOLAR SYSTEM

**The sun is 865,400 miles wide and at the center of the solar system.**

| | MERCURY | VENUS | EARTH | MARS | JUPITER |
|---|---|---|---|---|---|
| Diameter at equator —in miles | 3,032 | 7,519 | 7,926 | 4,194 | 88,736 |
| Distance from the sun—in millions of miles | 36 | 67 | 93 | 142 | 484 |

Size in the solar system is another measure that is hard to grasp. The sun, for instance, is 109 times larger than Earth. To appreciate this, line up 109 peas along a yardstick. They measure to about the thirty-two inch mark. Now hold up a single pea. That's the size of our planet compared to the sun, our star.

Try now to picture the solar system the same way. This will give an idea of the space between planets and the sun and also of the distances asteroids travel.

The sun in this example is the size of a six-inch grapefruit. Earth has shrunk to the size of an *o* in this sentence.

Place your grapefruit-sun on the goal line of the high school football field and start the planets in orbit. Mercury is seven yards away. Our *o*-sized Earth occupies a space on

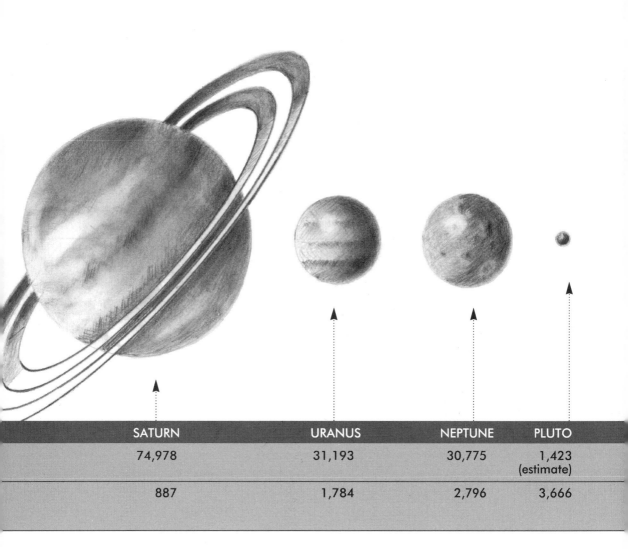

| SATURN | URANUS | NEPTUNE | PLUTO |
|--------|--------|---------|-------|
| 74,978 | 31,193 | 30,775 | 1,423 (estimate) |
| 887 | 1,784 | 2,796 | 3,666 |

the eighteen-yard line. Mars is on the twenty-eight-yard line, Jupiter on the ninety-five-yard line, almost to the opposite goal line. Far-off Pluto would require another six football fields to place it.

Between Mars and Jupiter, the asteroid belt occupies about twenty yards between the sixty- and eighty-yard lines.

This is the space—from the asteroid belt to the sun—in which most asteroids play. This is the awesome emptiness in which astronomers try to locate these flying rocks as they pass against a background of twinkling stars.

This is the void across which these space scientists may one day spot an asteroid heading for our tiny blue planet and make plans to intercept it.

# The Missing Planet

steroids have orbited the sun for more than 4 billion years, but astronomers discovered them only 200 years ago, and then by accident. This discovery had to do with a cosmic puzzle that had mystified astronomers for years. The puzzle involved a missing planet.

About 1774, Johann Bode, a German astronomer, wrote three sentences in the *Astronomical Yearbook* that expressed their puzzlement:

"Is it not probable that a planet actually revolved in the orbit which the finger of the Almighty had drawn for it? Can we believe that the Creator of the world left this space empty? Certainly not!"

Only eight years earlier, another German astronomer, Johann Titius, had worked out calculations to *prove* that another planet had to circle the sun at a distance of 260 million miles. But where was it?

What bothered Titius, Bode, and other astronomers was the large gap in space that existed between Mars and Jupiter. The six planets besides Earth that astronomers knew about—Mercury, Venus, Mars, Jupiter, Saturn, and Uranus (Neptune was discovered in 1846 and Pluto in 1930)—orbited the sun at regular intervals.

But there was space between Mars and Jupiter. Something seemed to be missing. For two centuries, this gap bothered astronomers. They knew where the missing planet should be. The problem was they couldn't see it through their telescopes.

So frustrating was the absence of a planet that in 1596, Johannes Kepler, a famous German astronomer, stated flatly, "Between Jupiter and Mars I place a planet!"

The solution to the puzzle came on January 1, 1801.

In Sicily, Giuseppi Piazzi, a teacher of mathematics at the University of Palermo, was preparing a new catalog of stars. Peering through the telescope in the university's observatory that night, he was astounded at what he saw. There was the planet astronomers had searched for and had never found. Moreover, it was exactly where it should be, in the space between Mars and Jupiter.

Piazzi was jubilant. He had discovered the missing planet! He named it Ceres Ferdinandea in honor of King Ferdinand III of Sicily. It was 620 miles wide, he said (about 135 miles too much, later measurements proved).

On the next night, again at his telescope, Piazzi had another surprise—a second planet in the Mars-Jupiter gap. On January 3, he found still another planet. Instead of one missing planet, he had found three! What was happening here?

Piazzi reviewed his data. Then he realized what he had seen; not major planets the size of the other six in the solar system, but three minor planets, asteroids. The term was an old Greek word. It meant "starlike" or "little stars." Piazzi had discovered the first asteroids ever seen from earth.

More sightings of asteroids in the Mars–Jupiter gap soon followed. German astronomer Heinrich Obers found one, 304 miles wide, in 1802 and named it Pallas. Other astronomers found Juno (118 miles wide) in 1804 and Vesta (243 miles wide) in 1807.

But astronomers weren't the only ones to discover asteroids. Amateur stargazers found them, too. In 1845, Karl Hencke, a postmaster in Prussia, spied Astraea. In Paris, a German painter named Goldschmidt set up a telescope in his apartment window above the Café Procope. While diners enjoyed chicken cooked in wine at the tables below, Goldschmidt discovered fourteen asteroids.

By the start of the twentieth century, more powerful telescopes found several hundred asteroids. Today, the orbits of about 19,000 have been tracked. Nearly all inhabit the asteroid belt between Mars and Jupiter.

Speeding along, rotating and tumbling in the cold space between the two planets, sometimes smashing together, most asteroids take about five years to make one lap around the distant sun.

# 6 Birth of the Asteroids

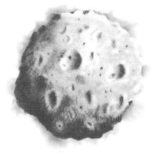

**W**here did asteroids come from?

At one time, astronomers believed that the asteroid belt consisted of rocks left over from a planet that had exploded.

Today, however, they believe just the opposite. Those flying stones and rocks, they say, are the building blocks of a planet that never managed to assemble itself—the missing planet that early astronomers searched for but never found.

Here is how astronomers today explain asteroids:

Some 4.6 billion years ago, the nine planets in our solar system began forming out of a thin disk of gas and dust revolving about the young sun. Like snowflakes, the specks of gas and dust clung together. Eventually enough specks gathered to compact into rock and, over millions of years, built into large planets.

During this building period, the gravity of four planets—Mercury, Venus, Earth, and Mars—swept up much of the rocky rubble in the inner solar system. The five remaining planets—Jupiter, Saturn, Uranus, Neptune, and Pluto—developed into gaseous planets. Whether made up of rock or gas, however, the nine planets formed at roughly regular intervals from the sun, except for one place: the space between Mars and Jupiter.

Here, the powerful gravity of Jupiter—at 88,736 miles wide the largest planet in the solar system (Earth is 7,926 miles wide)—was strong enough to prevent billions of stones and rocks, left over when the inner planets formed, from joining together into a tenth planet. Instead, these stones and rocks continued to circle the sun in a broad belt between Mars and Jupiter.

It's possible, some astronomers say, that the early asteroid belt was made up not of small stones and rocks, but of a half hundred large bodies 50 to 500 miles wide. Then these large bodies started crashing into one another. Left today from these collisions are a few large asteroids and billions of broken fragments traveling around the sun at a distance of 2.2 to 3.3 AU. (AU is a term that means astronomical unit, the distance from the sun to earth: 93 million miles.) Packing all asteroids together would make a ball a tenth of the mass of the moon, a tennis ball compared to a basketball. But that sphere probably would have been the size of the tenth planet if it had developed like the others.

Today, about 100,000 asteroids are bright enough, in the light from the faraway sun, to be photographed from Earth. About thirty to thirty-five so far discovered are wider than 125 miles. Another 11,000 to 12,000 have diameters larger than eighteen to twenty miles. A half million are a mile across. A million or so are at least a half mile in diameter.

Astronomers have given numbers or names to more than 6,000. Some are named for heroes in old Greek myths: Icarus, Hermes. Others honor astronomers: Kepler, Hale. Flower names are also popular: Crocus, Begonia. Cities: Yalta, Chicago. Women: Sheba, Dulcinea, Marlene.

Asteroids also come in many shapes. Eros is a spindle-shaped rock twenty-two miles long, ten miles wide, and

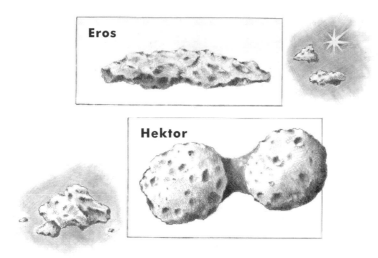

four miles thick, turning end over end. As it tumbles along in the asteroid belt, it also revolves—its day is five hours and sixteen minutes long.

Hektor is shaped like a dumbbell—two asteroids may have collided and remained together rather than bounding apart.

Other asteroids turn about each other or have smaller rocks orbiting around them. Some asteroids are dark red; others are black as charcoal. Many show low hills, deep valleys, and cracks, pits, and craters from impacts and collisions with other asteroids.

Asteroids come in many shapes and sizes. Spindle-shaped Eros is 22 miles long. Hektor, 186 miles long, may have formed its dumbbell profile when two asteroids collided at low speed and joined. Small asteroids are often fragments from collisions between larger asteroids.

### CALCULATE GASPRA'S SPIN RATE FOR EXTRA CREDIT

As a summer project in 1989, thirteen-year-old Claudine Madras, Newton, Massachusetts, worked with astronomer Richard Binzel, Massachusetts Institute of Technology, to determine the time for Gaspra to make one rotation around itself. Binzel showed Madras how to analyze light curves on photographs of the asteroid taken from earth. She also went to Lowell Observatory in Arizona to observe Gaspra through the 1.1-meter telescope. Her calculations not only determined Gaspra's spin rate—one turn in 7.04 hours—but also predicted its long shape. Her findings provided useful information to space scientists planning the *Galileo* flyby two years later. Here, Madras and Binzel examine a model of the asteroid.
Sky Publishing Company/J. Kelly Beatty

The first close-up photographs of an asteroid were taken on October 29, 1991. The *Galileo* space probe, bound for Jupiter, passed within 1,000 miles of the asteroid Gaspra.

The photos show a potato-shaped rock about twelve miles long and seven miles wide. Hundreds of craters pit its surface. Raw scrapes in places suggest glancing blows from other asteroids. A layer of dust or broken rock two to six feet deep may blanket its surface. Gaspra turns about itself every seven hours.

One astronomer who examined the photos said, "We suspect Gaspra is a survivor of a series of catastrophic collisions in which a succession of parent bodies got broken down into smaller and smaller pieces."

Distances among asteroids were confirmed when *Pioneer 10*, a space probe, was launched from Cape Kennedy in Florida on March 2, 1972. *Pioneer 10* crossed Mars's orbit on

May 25, entered the asteroid belt July 15, and passed the outer edge on February 15, 1973.

For seven long months, it sped through the belt at 30,000 miles per hour. The probe was a sizable object—a round dish antenna twelve feet wide sprouting booms, one forty-three feet long, hung with instruments.

Yet, for all its size, *Pioneer 10* never encountered an asteroid. Even a pebble-sized asteroid striking the craft could have disabled it. An impact detector on the antenna recorded not a single strike.

The largest asteroids—Ceres, 485 miles; Pallas, 304 miles; and Vesta, 243 miles—tend to be round. Over time, their own gravity pulled them together into a ball, a shape that balances itself. All nine planets in the solar system are ball-shaped.

Most rocks in the asteroid belt follow stable orbits—they continue along the same track just as they have for 4 billion years. Vesta—nearly 300 million miles from the sun and 127 million miles from earth—circles the sun in 3.63 Earth years. It rotates, just as Earth does. Its day is five hours, twenty-one minutes, compared with Earth's twenty-three-hour, fifty-six-minute day.

Collisions between asteroids often traveling at 11,000 miles per hour must be spectacular.

From a distance of 1,000 miles, the *Galileo* spacecraft radioed Gaspra's image back to earth in October 1991. More than 600 craters 330 to 1,650 feet pit the surface of this 12-by-7.5-by-7-mile asteroid. The largest crater measures 3.7 miles across. Within the asteroid belt, Gaspra circles the sun at a distance of 205 million miles.
NASA

A broken fragment may continue along the same orbit as the parent asteroid or it may fly out of the asteroid belt into a new orbit. The new orbit may take it around earth or one of the other planets in the inner solar system. Or it may be drawn into the fiery furnace of the sun. Still other fragments may go the other way, flying off into deep space. Often fragments remaining from a collision cluster again, drawn together by their mutual gravity.

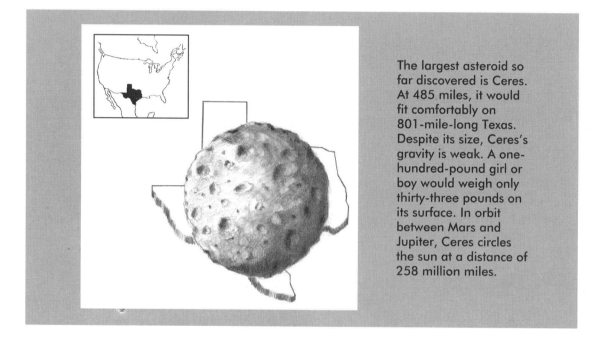

The largest asteroid so far discovered is Ceres. At 485 miles, it would fit comfortably on 801-mile-long Texas. Despite its size, Ceres's gravity is weak. A one-hundred-pound girl or boy would weigh only thirty-three pounds on its surface. In orbit between Mars and Jupiter, Ceres circles the sun at a distance of 258 million miles.

Astronomers estimate that one out of every five asteroids ejected from the asteroid belt begins an orbit around the sun. In their long flights, some—about fifteen new asteroids every million years—cross the path of Earth, joining others already crossing Earth's orbit. These are the asteroids, the Earth-crossers, that astronomers today search for in the night skies.

# 7 Dead Comets

About thirty comets pass inside Earth's orbit each year. Unlike asteroids, comets can often be seen through telescopes or binoculars. They show a glowing tail, much like a searchlight, as they cruise through the night sky.

Astronomers call them "dirty snowballs." Another name might be "frozen dirtballs." Studies show a comet's nucleus, or core, to be made up of ice, rocky dust particles, and frozen gas. It is usually a few miles wide.

Like asteroids, comets orbit the sun, but at greater distances. Consider this: Pluto, the outermost planet, is 3,666 million miles from the sun. The Oort cloud, where comets roam, is halfway to the nearest star, 3,720 trillion miles from the sun.

How to imagine such a distance? Light from the sun travels at 186,000 miles per second. It crosses the 93-million-mile space to Earth in a little more than eight minutes. To cross the thousands of miles to the Oort cloud, however, takes the same light 231 days. That gives an idea of the

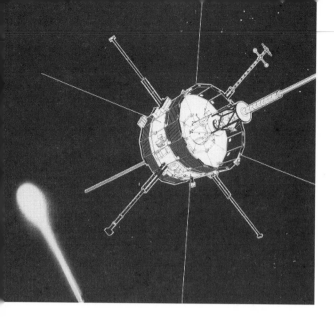

In 1985, the *International Sun-Earth Explorer* passed through the tail of comet Giacobini-Zinner (bottom right), the first spacecraft to do so. Scientists have now examined particles—smaller than a ten-thousandth of a centimeter— suspected to have come from its tail (below). Study of comet cores and tails helps astronomers learn how the solar system began and evolved.
NASA/JPL

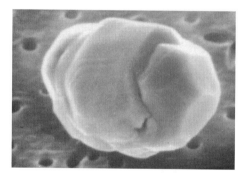

awesome distance comets travel to reach our sun and our planet.

The Oort cloud was named after the Dutch astronomer Jan Oort, who discovered it in 1950. In the cloud that surrounds the sun at a distance of 40,000 AU, Oort said, a hundred billion iceballs mill about at 300 miles per hour in "cold storage."

Like asteroids, comets are made up of the raw materials left over from the whirling clouds of gas and dust that created the solar system 4.6 billion years ago. "If you want to study the beginning of the solar system," said an astronomer, "comets are your best bet."

How do comets leave the faraway Oort cloud and travel the vast distance to the inner solar system?

Oort said that now and then a far-off star passing close to the cloud is the cause. The star's gravity slows a few iceballs to a mere five to ten miles per hour, about the speed of a leisurely pedaled bicycle. As the comets slow, the sun's gravity begins to tug at them. Suddenly hundreds of iceballs leave the cloud and begin to "fall" toward the sun.

By the time an iceball passes Jupiter and Mars and is visible from earth, it is racing at tremendous speed, some 90,000 to 100,000 miles per hour.

The sun's warmth turns the frozen surface gases into vapor, which boils off the core in a glowing tail. As it circles the sun and starts its return trip, a comet's speed may increase to 1 million miles per hour.

The comet's tail streams particles of water vapor, frozen gas (oxygen and hydrogen among other gases), dust bits, and crumbs of rock for millions of miles. In 1973, comet Kohoutek streamed a tail 3 million miles long, actually a mere stub of a tail compared with those of some comets. When Earth passes through a trail of comet litter, the rocky grains burn bright as they fall through the atmosphere. We call this rain of comet debris a "meteor shower."

Live comets follow cosmic timetables, like bus schedules, although they are frequently early or late. Halley's comet, the best known, reappears in our skies every seventy-five to seventy-six years. In between Earth passes, it travels far out beyond Pluto before swinging back again.

In 1986, astronomers in forty-seven countries watched the comet streak through the night sky at 100,000 miles per hour. Five satellites in orbit above Earth signaled that the peanut-shaped core was nine miles long and four to six miles wide. Specks of dust and gas boiled off its surface to form a glowing tail 100 million miles long.

Each pass around the sun takes a toll on a comet. In time, all frozen gas, surface dust, and rock burn off. Then the comet "dies" and may become an asteroid. While one hundred new comets enter the inner solar system each year, ten times as many burned-out comet cores continue on their timeless paths.

Still, comets or comet cores that approach earth may not actually strike the surface. Instead, scientists say, they vaporize from the friction of the atmosphere and blow up in spectacular blasts before hitting the ground.

Sir Edmund Halley (1656–1742) was the first astronomer to predict the return of a comet. After calculating the orbit of the great comet of 1682 —since known as Halley's comet— he claimed it was the same comet that had streaked by Earth in 1531 and 1607, and that it would return again in early 1759. Sky watchers also sighted the comet in 1835, 1910, and 1986. On a regular flyby schedule of seventy-five to seventy-six years, Halley's comet is next expected in 2061. NASA/JPL

No evidence of a comet impact has ever been found on Earth. But a possible comet air blast may have occurred on the night of April 9, 1984. The crews of several airliners flying over the North Pacific Ocean were startled to see a mushroom cloud suddenly soar 70,000 feet high and spread 200 miles.

Scientists investigating the incident stated that the crews had witnessed a rare event, a dead-comet core exploding as it entered moisture-laden clouds high above the ocean.

Dead comet cores have appeared in the past. In 1949, a comet registered, but only feebly, on a photographic plate during a sky survey at Palomar Observatory in southern California. In 1979, Eleanor Helin identified the comet, now burned out, only its dead core remaining, as an asteroid. Over this thirty-year period the comet had evolved into an asteroid.

The possibility of a comet impact on earth, however, was once thought possible. In 1962, comet Swift-Tuttle passed earth at a distance of 50 million miles, roughly halfway to the sun, close but not a threat. In 1992, it passed again at a safe distance.

But for the year 2126, calculations showed its flight would bring it close to Earth. An impact was even thought possible. Then, new observations of the comet's path resulted in "the prediction being withdrawn."

There are many unanswered questions about comets and how they behave, astronomers say. The gas and dust boiling off a comet's core over billions of miles of space may gradually change its speed and orbit. Perhaps this is what caused astronomers to conclude that earth will be spared an impact with Swift-Tuttle in that far distant year.

In 1986, Halley's comet sped by Earth at a distance of 38.8 million miles. The glowing "head," or coma, of a comet can measure thousands of miles across, although the comet's core may be only a few miles wide. Gas and dust flow from the icy core in a long tail that always points away from the sun. As a comet circles the sun and heads for the outer solar system, it chases its own tail.
NOAA

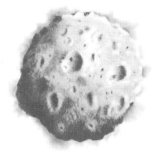

In the past, earth scientists say, asteroids struck the Earth far more often than today. As the young Earth formed and grew, it pulled in leftover chunks of rock not used in building other planets.

In the first 700 million years, our planet may have been bombarded almost daily with rocks from space; its surface looked much like the surface of the moon today, cratered and pockmarked.

Look at the moon through a six-inch telescope and you can see these ancient craters. In places, they appear shoulder to shoulder, younger craters overlapping older craters. A count of craters on the visible side of the moon reveals five large craters forty-five miles wide, twenty-four more with diameters of fifteen to thirty miles, and thousands of smaller craters, football field size down to a few feet. The surface of the moon is a three-foot-deep layer of churned-up soil from the pounding of incoming space rocks.

Other planets in the solar system also show evidence of this early bombardment. Mercury, Venus, and Mars are pitted with craters. So are the moons of Jupiter and Saturn.

A crater on another planet appears exactly as it did when an asteroid hit. But Earth craters undergo enormous change because of our planet's atmosphere. Across 4 billion years, wind and rain have scoured the land, erasing the craters. Mountain ranges have raised and lowered, destroying the craters. Oceans occupy what was once dry land, hiding craters. Meteor Crater in Arizona is young in earth terms but already shows the wear of 500 centuries of weather.

**MOON.** The surface is pockmarked with millions of craters punched into the soil by impacting meteorites. Since the moon has no air or water to cause erosion, the craters remain as they were when formed. In the background is the large crater called Copernicus. NASA

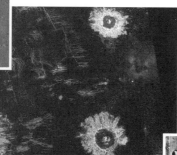

**VENUS.** Three large impact craters on the second planet from the sun range from twenty-three to thirty-one miles. Bright material around each rim is surface soil thrown from the crater by the impact of the meteorite. Sloping inner walls and central peaks also suggest meteorite strikes. NASA

**MARS.** Fifteen photos at a distance of 1,040 miles were combined to form this image of the surface of the fourth planet from the sun. The area shown is 155 by 120 miles. Lava flows, broken by gashes and ridges, are peppered with meteorite impact craters. NASA

Despite these alterations by the weather, however, scientists can identify craters left by objects striking Earth hundreds of thousands—even millions—of years in the past. About 150 craters have been found, and the list grows by five or six each year. Estimates are that a thousand more await discovery. The largest found so far, in Ontario, Canada, is 124 miles rim to rim.

Some other large craters:

- Vredefort Dome in South Africa, eighty-seven miles wide.
- The bowl of Lake Bosumtwi in Ghana, Africa. At 1.3 million years, perhaps the youngest crater larger than six miles.
- Lake Manicouagan in northeastern Quebec, Canada. The lake is forty-four miles wide inside a crater sixty miles across and more than 200 million years old.
- Ries Basin, seventeen miles wide, in southern Germany north of Augsburg. Fifteen million years ago, an object from space, a mile wide with a mass of a billion tons, struck the area and blasted out a mass of rock three-miles deep. Today, the basin is home to several villages and the old city of Nordlingen. Around the rim are broken and upended rocks.
- Three hundred million years ago, an asteroid left an eight-mile-wide crater sixty-eight miles south of present-day Chicago.
- Sixty-five million years ago, an asteroid traveling ten to twenty miles each second blasted a hole twenty-five miles wide that today lies under cornfields near Manson, Iowa.

**CLEARWATER LAKES.** Two meteorites created these twin crater lakes 290 million years ago in Quebec, Canada. The ten-mile-wide lake—with islands—today fills a crater that originally measured twenty-two miles. The crater of the small lake was originally fifteen miles wide. NASA

How do scientists know these craters were caused by objects from space crashing into Earth? Maybe the craters are just old volcanoes.

# EARTH'S SCARS

More than 130 large meteorite craters have been discovered on earth's surface. Most are located in populated areas where scientists are likely to recognize the huge bowls in the land. Many more impact craters probably exist but haven't been found. They are likely hidden at the bottom of the sea, in the rain forests of South America, and in the jungles of Southeast Asia. At one time, the young earth was probably as heavily cratered as the moon. But shifting landmasses, mountain building, and the wearing away of craters by water and wind over million of years erased this evidence of past meteorite strikes on our planet. *All Photographs courtesy of NASA.*

**Kara Kul.** The diameter of this crater three and a half miles high in the Pamir Mountain Range near Afghanistan is twenty-eight miles. The lake that fills it is sixteen miles wide. Only recently has rock, deformed and mashed by the impact of a meteorite 10 million years ago, been found.

**Bosumtwi.** A lake now fills a 7-mile-wide, 1.3-million-year-old impact crater in Ghana, west-central Africa. Clouds partly hide the lake in this photo taken from space by the space shuttle. The original crater, altered by erosion, was smaller, 6.5 miles.

Atlantic Ocean

Pacific Ocean

Indian Ocean

Pacific Ocean

**Manicouagan.** About 210 million years old, this impact crater in Quebec, Canada, was originally nearly sixty-two miles wide, but glaciers spreading repeatedly over the region filled in much of the original crater. A ring lake forty-three miles wide remains today.

**Wolf Creek.** Located in north-central Australia, the rim of this half-mile-wide crater rises 82 feet above the desert plain. The floor is 164 feet below the rim. Fragments of the iron meteorite that struck 300,000 years ago and bits of impact glass have been found at the site.

Meteor Crater in Arizona showed earth scientists the
way to identify strikes by space objects.

One clue was found in specimens of quartz. Grains of
this hard mineral had been compressed to one-
third their normal size. Only something like an
object weighing 300,000 tons striking the
area at 43,000 miles per hour could have
produced the enormous pressure necessary
to compress quartz grains. (Shocked quartz
is also found at nuclear bomb sites in
Nevada. The blasts fuse sand grains into
quartz crystals.)

Another clue was tektites, glassy bits created
by the impact of the space rock. Beneath the crater
floor and for miles around the blast site, scientists found
these glassy bodies an inch in size or smaller and microscopic spheres of melted iron.

Rare metals in rock ejected from the crater provided
another clue. Searchers found particles of platinum, iridium,
and gold. These metals are abundant in space rocks but
rare in surface rocks on earth.

Besides these clues, the crater itself was evidence of an
enormous impact. Rock and dirt blasted skyward as the
asteroid struck, creating a cone or funnel of the ejected
rock and soil around the rim of the crater. Drops of iron
from the asteroid rained down on the surrounding plain. In
the case of Meteor Crater, these droplets have been found
as far away as eleven miles.

Finally, searchers found fragments of the asteroid itself.
These pieces broke off the parent rock as it plunged
through the atmosphere. The largest chunk found near
Meteor Crater weighed 1,406 pounds.

Searchers have
found tektites—
tiny, glassy
kernels instantly
created in the
white-hot heat
of a large
meteorite's smash
into Earth—in and
around impact
craters. The round
tektite at left
in this photo
measures about
three-fourths
of an inch.
Geological Survey of
Canada (GSC 203031-B)

Everglades National Park at the southern tip of Florida may have been created by the impact of a massive asteroid 38 million years ago. Today, tourists visit the vast, trackless swamp of the Everglades to marvel at the variety of wildlife that resides there.
Florida Department of Commerce, Division of Tourism

Craters in other parts of the world show the same signs—rock compressed and deformed by the enormous heat and pressure of an impact, microscopic bits of iron and glass, particles of rare metals, a raised rim of broken rocks around the crater. All became evidence of an impact by an object hurtling in from space and striking our planet.

One suspected crater scientists are studying is the site of Everglades National Park on the southern tip of Florida.

A 5,000-square-mile subtropical swamp the size of Connecticut, the Everglades is the largest of all U.S. wetlands, home to herons, panthers, alligators, and scores of other birds, mammals, and reptiles. Containing the watery black muck of the swamp is a bowl-like limestone basin about thirty-five miles southwest of present-day Miami. In the 1940s, geologists probed the "basement" under the swamp and found a network of fractures—breaks— in the limestone. These breaks radiated from a central point like cracks in a pane of glass struck by a stone. Scientific instruments detected metal under the muck of the swamp.

What created the basin? Why does metal underlie the swamp? In 1985, new studies suggested the answer.

Some 38 million years ago, the new theory said, an asteroid, part stone and part metal, slammed into the area, then covered by 600 feet of ocean, and punched a hole in the seabed, fracturing the rock.

In time, coral reefs grew along the raised rim of the basin created by the impact and eventually—4 to 6 million years ago—the reefs rose above the water's surface, joined the mainland, and closed out the ocean. Rivers flowed into the basin and created a huge freshwater lake.

The rivers also carried mud and sand into the basin. In time, this sediment nearly filled the lake. Lake Okeechobee in southern Florida is the last of the original inland lake. Under the warm tropical sun, a broad swamp thrived, the present-day Everglades.

Not all earth scientists agree that the Everglades grew from this series of events. But as research continues in the region, many believe that an asteroid will be shown to have started events that led to the magnificent Everglades we know today.

Perhaps the strangest story of an asteroid colliding with our planet, however, concerns the birth of the moon. The "giant-impact" theory suggests an astonishing idea: that the moon was created from the earth in one of the most stunning collisions in the history of the solar system.

When Earth was young, the theory goes, a giant body half its size—possibly as large as 4,200-mile-wide Mars—struck earth at 26,000 miles per hour. So violent was the collision that the massive asteroid was completely vaporized.

Rock and dust blasted through the air blanket around Earth and went into orbit. There, this rubble gathered into a thin ring. In the same process that formed the asteroids and planets, the stronger gravity of large chunks pulled in small chunks. Across a few million years, the pieces assembled into the moon, orbiting Earth at a distance of only 15,000 miles. Another few million years passed and the moon gradually spiraled outward to its present position 240,000 miles away.

Where is the crater left by the monster asteroid? Immediately after the impact, liquid rock from deep within the earth flowed into the wound. Within hours, the crater filled and Earth again took the shape of a globe. All evidence of the stupendous impact that created the moon had vanished.

# Stones from Heaven

**T**oday, large asteroids striking earth are rare, perhaps because the solar system is more stable and large asteroids stay in steady orbit in the asteroid belt.

Smaller stones, however, continue to pelt the earth—about 20,000 tons enter the atmosphere each year. Most are the size of pinheads and burn up before striking the ground. But about one hundred tons of stones weighing a few ounces to a ton or more also arrive each year. One researcher says meteorites about the size of apples strike earth once every two hours, but few people ever see it happen.

Meteor, meteoroid, and meteorite are terms that are often confused. They are all bits and pieces of larger asteroids. However, astronomers call them "meteoroids" when they leave the asteroid belt and speed through space, "meteors" when they enter Earth's atmosphere and become fireballs or shooting stars, and "meteorites" when they hit the ground.

Scientists did not always believe that stones fell from the sky. That idea began with a German scientist, Ernst Chiadni. In 1794, Chiadni published a report that said meteorites were stones from space, leftovers from when the planets formed. Chiadni was far ahead of his time, but no one took his strange ideas seriously.

In America about the same year, two professors from Yale University told President Thomas Jefferson that meteorites fell onto earth from space. Jefferson, one of the most learned men of his day, scoffed. "I would prefer to believe that two Yankee professors would lie rather than that stones could fall from heaven."

Then an event occurred that made believers out of the doubters. On April 26, 1803, a fireball streaked high over western France. Observers watched as the fireball broke apart and several thousand stones showered down.

The fireball convinced scientists. Stones did indeed rain from the sky! But why from the sky? They pointed to the moon. Stones were ejected from volcanoes on that heavenly body, they said, and fell to earth.

Over many years, however, as meteorites were collected and studied, that idea was gradually discarded. Stones from the sky, scientists confirmed, were meteorites, rocks left over from the time the planets formed.

The largest known meteorite found on earth today is the Hoba West in Namibia in southwest Africa near the town of Grootfontein.

Found in 1920, the Hoba West is dark and rusty looking, 9 by 9 by 3 feet, and weighs sixty-six tons. A meteorite like the Hoba West that contains iron is stronger than a meteorite that is entirely stone. That is probably the reason why the Hoba West resisted breaking up in its heated passage through the atmosphere to its resting place on the Hoba farm.

The second largest known meteorite is the Ahnighito— Eskimo for "tent"—found in western Greenland. Eskimo hunters hammered off chunks to shape into harpoon tips and knife blades.

In 1897, Arctic explorer Robert E. Peary had the thirty-four-ton rock hauled 300 feet to the shore where his ship waited. After circling in the asteroid belt for millions of years, Ahnighito now rests in the Arthur Ross Hall of Meteorites in the American Museum of Natural History in New York. Tests showed the space rock to be 4.5 billion years old, just about the age of earth.

An even older space visitor was found near the village of Allende in northwestern Mexico. At 1 A.M. on February 8, 1969, villagers watched a meteor burn blue-white

Belts of chains hold the thirty-four-ton iron meteorite —named Ahnighito by Eskimos—to the deck of explorer Robert E. Peary's ship near Cape York, Greenland. Peary transported the rock, thought to have fallen to earth 10,000 years earlier, to New York in 1897. American Museum of Natural History (#329148)

In 1902, this pitted and cavernous 14.1-ton iron meteorite fell to earth in the Cascade Range of mountains two miles northwest of Willamette, Oregon. The main mass and pieces were distributed among twelve museums and universities for examination and study.
Smithsonian Institution, National Museum of Natural History

across the night sky. As it fell, the meteor broke up in a spectacular display of fireworks and scattered small chunks across an area ten miles square. The largest piece weighed two tons. It was named the Allende.

A scientist who examined the rock found clumps of minerals clustered like raisins in a cupcake. "Some of these minerals condensed from the original gases that created the sun and planets," he said. "They haven't changed since then." Allende's age was determined to be 4.6 billion years.

Meteorites seem to arrive at unexpected times.

On the outskirts of Holbrook, Arizona, one afternoon in 1912, a family was eating dinner when they heard a "terrific crash" outside. Dashing from the house, one boy called, "It's raining rocks out here!"

Puffs of dust spurting on a mile of plain made the family think of "bullets kicking up dust." A shower of 14,000 meteorites had just arrived from space. The family collected all they could find—481 pounds of space rocks.

On July 6, 1924, as a funeral was being conducted in a cemetery behind a church in Johnston, Colorado, mourners heard a sound like machine-

A stony meteorite found near Abee, Alberta, Canada. Angular in shape, it shows a pebbly surface, shallow pits, and a smooth black fusion crust created by the heat of its passage through the atmosphere. Weight: 211.5 pounds. Size: 12 by 16 by 19 inches.

Geological Survey of Canada (GSC 109341-B)

gun fire. Then a meteorite the size of a football hit the dirt road nearby. After the service, the funeral director dug it out.

In 1971 and again in 1982, meteorites crashed through the roofs of houses in Wethersfield, Connecticut. People in the houses were mighty surprised, but unhurt.

On January 6, 1985, the Rios family near La Criolla, Argentina, heard a sonic boom before a fifteen-pound meteorite plunged through the roof of their farm home and smashed a door. The meteorite had broken up in its downward plunge through the atmosphere. The family reported that they had been terrified, but no one was hurt.

The Casas Grandes iron meteorite was found in an ancient tomb in 1867 near Chihuahua in northern Mexico near the Texas–New Mexico border and presented to the Smithsonian Institution nine years later in 1876. Original weight before fragments chipped off for study: 3,407 pounds. Smithsonian Institution, National Museum of Natural History

Brodie Spaulding, Noblesville, Indiana, shows the meteorite that fell in his front yard in August 1991. Researchers believe the rock is 4.5 billion years old and may have come from the interior of an asteroid. Only about ten meteorites like Brodie's have been found.
THE DAILY LEDGER, Noblesville, Ind./Gregg R. Montgomery; NASA, Johnson Space Center

Has anyone ever been hit by a meteorite falling from the sky? Consider these cases:

On April 28, 1927, in Aba, Japan, a five-year-old girl playing in the garden of her home suddenly cried out. Her mother found a meteorite "the size of a kidney bean" in the girl's neckband. After its long flight to earth, the stone now rests in a museum in Japan. Its name: the Aba.

November 30, 1954. High over Alabama, an army pilot saw a white streak in the night sky, like a falling star. It seemed to be heading toward the town of Sylacauga. In town, Ms. E. Huiitt Hodges was sleeping on the sofa in the living room of her home across from the Comet Drive-In Theatre. A loud crash awakened her. At first, she thought the gas heater had exploded. Then she felt a sharp pain in her hip. On the rug before her startled eyes was the cause of the pain: an eight-and-a-half-pound rock. A meteorite had plunged through the roof, bounced off the radio, and struck her hip, leaving a nasty bruise.

These two instances are the only ones known of meteorites actually hitting anyone. (In a meteor shower of forty stones that fell near Alexandria, Egypt, on the morning of June 28, 1911, one stone was said to have killed a wandering dog.) But others have come close.

Much too close, thirteen-year-old Brodie Spaulding of Noblesville, Indiana, might have said.

On August 31, 1991, about 7 P.M., while Brodie was in his front yard, he heard a "low whistle" and then a thud. Turning, he saw a fist-sized meteorite on the grass about twelve feet away. The impact left a crater four inches wide and about an inch and a half deep. The rock, crusty black and brown, was still warm when Brodie picked it up.

"I was amazed," he said later. "It just happened all of a sudden. It was kind of scary. I feel pretty lucky, especially because it didn't hit me."

A meteorite specialist at Purdue University weighed the rock: one pound, three ounces.

"Only about one of these falls on every million square kilometers on the earth's surface each year," he said. "It's very rare to have one fall at someone's feet."

# Disappearing Dinosaurs

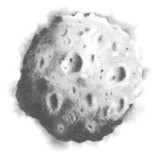

One of the great mysteries of science began with an event that happened 65 million years ago. Earth then was a far different place from what it is today. No humans lived here. The weather was warm and damp, and dinosaurs trod the land.

Then something extraordinary happened. After 140 million years of living on the planet, the dinosaurs suddenly disappeared. Along with the dinosaurs, nearly all small animals and most trees and plants also disappeared. Dinosaur bones 144 million to 65 million years old have been found, but not a single bone younger than 65 million years.

For years, the mystery baffled scientists. Maybe the climate changed, they said, and became too hot or too cold, and the big beasts couldn't stand it. Another idea: Small animals ate eggs laid by the dinosaurs. With no offspring to carry on the species, they simply died out. Or perhaps poisonous plants or deadly diseases caused them to disappear.

These ideas were carefully discussed, but they over-looked something. All suggested a gradual dying out of the great beasts when, in fact, their disappearance was relatively sudden and complete.

Years of pondering the mystery provided no satisfactory answer. And then, on January 4, 1980, Luis Alvarez, a scientist at the University of California, appeared at a meeting of the American Association for the Advancement of Science in San Francisco.

Before the group of scientists, Alvarez made a startling announcement: He knew what had happened 65 million years ago to wipe out the dinosaurs and most other animals and plants on Earth!

Not all scientists who heard Alvarez that day agreed with him. But a growing body of evidence seems to support his ideas. Here is how he explained the mysterious disap-pearance of the dinosaurs.

In the spring of 1977, Alvarez's son, Walter, was exam-ining a strange layer of reddish brown clay near the town of Gubbio in the mountains one hundred miles north of Rome, Italy. Walter was a geologist, a scientist who studies rocks.

Dinosaurs occupied our planet for 140 million years before they suddenly disappeared 65 million years ago. An asteroid —or comet— may have caused their extinction. Here, fierce tyrannosaurus, forty feet from jaws to tip of tail, confronts three-horned triceratops, ready to defend itself. American Museum of Natural History (#129205)

Walter noticed something odd about the clay. It was a half inch to an inch thick and sandwiched between layers of pink and white limestone. Fossils—traces of animals and plants once buried and hardened into rock—above and below the clay layer showed that many animals had disappeared when the clay was deposited.

Laboratory tests revealed that the clay was 65 million years old and contained a rare metal, iridium—thirty times more iridium than in the limestone above and below.

Iridium is silvery gray in color. It is related to gold and platinum in the family of rare metals. Special about iridium is that it is found in only three places: 2,000 miles

Near Gubbio, Italy, Luis and Walter Alvarez stand at the dark clay seam, between layers of limestone, that provided the clue to how the dinosaurs may have disappeared. Many scientists believe the iridium-rich clay is the fallout of dust particles blasted into the atmosphere 65 million years ago by the impact of a six-mile-wide asteroid, a time that meshed with the disappearance of the dinosaurs. Each inch of limestone required 2,000 years to build. The coin is the size of a twenty-five cent piece. University of California, Lawrence Berkeley Laboratory

underground, in the cosmic dust that settles on Earth from exploding meteors and comets, and in meteorites striking Earth.

Led by Walter Alvarez, teams of scientists found similar layers of iridium-rich clay in Spain, New Zealand, and New Mexico. In Denmark, the clay layer was 160 times richer in iridium than in the surrounding rock. Since then, the clay with iridium has been found in more than one hundred places worldwide.

Where had this strange layer of clay come from? Why did it contain such a high amount of iridium when layers of rock on either side lacked this same metal?

On that January day in 1980, Luis Alvarez gave an answer that stunned his fellow scientists.

Sixty-five million years ago, he said, an asteroid six miles in diameter struck Earth. It hit at 45,000 miles per hour with the force of a hundred million nuclear bombs.

The impact punched a hole 120 miles wide and blasted 4 trillion tons of dirt and rock into the sky. High winds carried the ejected dirt and dust across the ocean. Airborne embers from burning trees started gigantic forest fires raging on every continent. Soot added to the dust cloud and blocked the sun's rays. Light on Earth was only a tenth of full moonlight.

The firestorm lasted until all trees and woody plants were used up. The darkness lasted for—how long? Six to nine months is one estimate. Another is three to five years. Deprived of the sun's warmth, Earth's temperature dropped to zero. Plants withered and died.

"Sunlight! That was the key," Luis Alvarez said. Without sunlight, plants stopped growing. Animals had no food to eat. Plant-eating dinosaurs starved. Then the meat-eating dinosaurs died. Only small mammals, birds, and reptiles survived by feeding on nuts, buried seeds, insects, and decaying plants.

The blanket of dust around the planet slowly drifted onto the continents and the oceans, a layer half inch to an inch thick rich in iridium from the destroyed asteroid. Luis Alvarez calculated that to spread that amount of iridium over the entire planet would have required an asteroid ten kilometers wide, a little more than six miles.

Alvarez's answer to what happened to the dinosaurs sounded probable, but something was missing: the crater. Although earth scientists had found scores of impact craters, a big crater 110 to 120 miles across and 65 million years old had not been found. The crater under cornfields near Manson, Iowa, showed promise. It was the right age, 65 million years, but too small—only twenty-five miles wide—for the impact of a six-mile-wide asteroid.

Then again, the six-mile-wide asteroid might have hit in the ocean—a likely possibility because seventy out of every one hundred miles of the Earth's surface is water. The crater, then, could be hidden at the bottom of the sea and more difficult to find.

Walter Alvarez said, "Many of us were thinking we'd never find it."

Then something unexpected happened.

Geologists looking for oil on Mexico's Yucatán Peninsula discovered a ring-shaped crater a mile underground. A satellite orbiting Earth, *Landsat 5,* showed evidence on the surface of the crater's rim, fractured rock. The rim measured 120 to 130 miles and extended underwater. The "bull's-eye" view of the crater was the village of Chicxulub on the shore of the Gulf of Mexico.

In 1992, rock in the crater was tested. Age of the crater: 64.98 million years!

Oil drills brought shocked quartz crystals and the telltale teardrop shapes of melted rock to the surface.

Since much of the Yucatán Peninsula was under 500 feet of water 65 million years ago, the asteroid must have sent up a gigantic wave when it struck. The asteroid was six miles wide—more than 30,000 feet. Its impact would have blasted rock from the bottom of the sea.

In Mexico, on the Caribbean Islands, in northern South America, and along the coast of Texas, searchers found broken rocks often five feet in diameter. In Cuba, the rocks formed a ridge 300 miles long and 500 yards thick. The rocks and the distance from Chicxulub indicated a wave three miles high had flung them for hundreds of miles.

On the southern shore of Haiti, scientists located the clay layer rich in iridium. It also contained shocked quartz grains, small beads of greenish black glass pellets, and grains of rock from the ocean floor.

Did the killer asteroid break apart in its plunge toward Earth? If so, a smaller chunk may have struck at Manson,

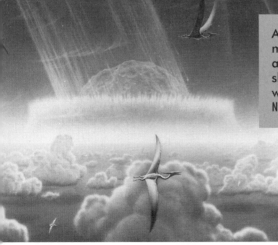

An asteroid crashing into earth 65 million years ago may have caused the extinction of the dinosaurs. In this artist's drawing, a six-mile-wide asteroid smashes into a shallow tropical sea as pterodactyls—flying reptiles with wingspans up to twenty feet—soar nearby. NASA

Iowa, and dug out the twenty-five-mile-wide crater, since it, too, had hit 65 million years ago.

As evidence for the asteroid impact in the Yucatán continues to mount, the Alvarez explanation of how the dinosaurs disappeared has gained many supporters.

But a 65-million-year-old mystery doesn't lend itself to easy solution. Scientists have learned to be cautious about supporting any theory until it can be proved without question. Was it really an asteroid that killed off the dinosaurs? Or was there another cause? Two other theories suggest that the cause might have been comets.

The first is the Planet X theory, which requires a tenth planet, so far undiscovered.

Scientists who support this theory say that this mystery planet orbits the sun once in 800 to 1,000 years. But its orbit is not regular; it changes. Every 28 million years, Planet X charges through the Oort cloud and dislodges

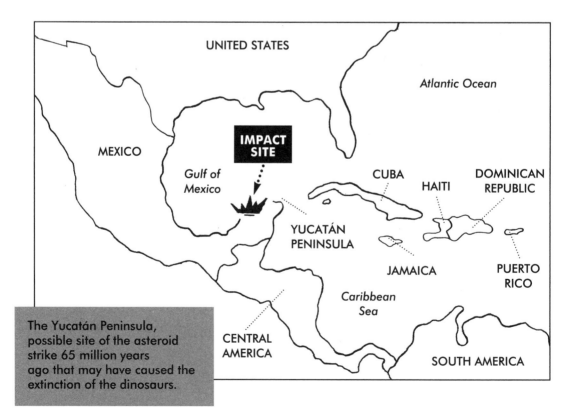

The Yucatán Peninsula, possible site of the asteroid strike 65 million years ago that may have caused the extinction of the dinosaurs.

hundreds of comets. Some of the dirty iceballs head for the sun. Their paths cross that of earth. Out of this gang of comets, one with a core six miles wide could have collided with earth 65 million years ago.

The second theory is Nemesis—the Death Star. A tiny, dim star, so far undiscovered, orbits the sun in a lopsided path.

Once every 26 million years, it plunges deep into the Oort cloud and dislodges a billion or so comets, some of which head for Earth. The next passage of the Death Star through the Oort cloud will be 15 million years from now, say scientists who support the theory.

Both the Planet X and Death Star theories have their supporters, but most scientists today say the Alvarez theory of an asteroid colliding with Earth is the "major contender" for the disappearance of the dinosaurs.

Whatever theory proves correct, however, one thing is for sure: Chance played a large part in the passing of the dinosaurs. If the asteroid—or comet—had crossed Earth's orbit just a half hour earlier or later, it would have passed safely by and gone zinging off into space. If so, the history of our planet would have been entirely different.

Scientists who study dinosaurs say that, at the time of the catastrophe 65 million years ago, some small dinosaurs had achieved a relationship of brain weight to body weight similar to some early mammals.

If that trend had continued and their offspring had developed intelligence, dinosaurs might have prevented the rise of human beings. A form of dinosaur might have survived to dominate the planet.

Our own position on the planet as the creature with the smartest brain might have taken a far different turn. An asteroid—maybe a comet—made the difference.

# Loose Cannonballs 11

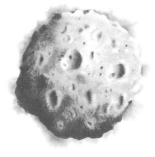

Astronomers say that an asteroid six miles wide collides with Earth only once in 100 million years. Despite these long odds, scientists take the threat of a major earth-asteroid collision very seriously.

Earth-crossing asteroids were first identified in 1932. In that year, Karl Reinmuth, an astronomer in Heidelberg, Germany, found the first Earth-crosser. Reinmuth was examining a photograph taken through a telescope when he saw something strange—a bright line among the stars.

Reinmuth identified the white line as an asteroid, a mile wide, passing Earth. He named it Apollo. Forty-one years later, in 1973, the same asteroid was seen again, a bright streak passing far from Earth in a moonless sky.

On October 28, 1937, Reinmuth found a second Earth-crosser. This asteroid, named Hermes, brushed by Earth at 22,000 miles per hour a mere 485,000 miles away, twice the distance from Earth to the moon, a mere whisker in astronomical terms. Two-thirds of a mile wide, Hermes could have exploded with a force of 100,000 nuclear bombs had it collided with Earth. Hermes then disappeared into space. Unfortunately, its orbit was not tracked.

By 1992, astronomers had discovered 150 Earth-crossing asteroids, including two bruisers about six miles wide, Sisyphus and Hephaistos. But they estimated there were between 1,500 and 2,000 larger than a half mile, all of whose paths crossed that of Earth. Any of these asteroids could collide with our planet.

"Loose cannonballs," they were called.

In recent years, astronomers have begun to record earth's close encounters with these "cannonballs."

• In the late 1960s, a mysterious explosion occurred over the South Atlantic Ocean. The blast had the power of a half-megaton bomb—500,000 tons of TNT. The U.S. Air Force thought a nuclear bomb had exploded. Later, investigators concluded that "a meteoroid—small asteroid—had blown up as it entered the atmosphere over this remote stretch of ocean."

• In 1969, Geographos passed within 5.6 million miles of Earth. Discovered in 1951, the cigar-shaped asteroid is two and a half miles long, a half mile wide, and tumbles end over end.

• On August 10, 1972, in broad daylight, witnesses saw a fireball trailing smoke streak across the sky from Utah north to Alberta, Canada. Some viewers heard a sonic boom. An Earth-circling satellite high above the fireball measured its speed at 31,000 miles per hour and its height above east-central Idaho at nearly thirty-six miles.

Although the meteorite passed too quickly for accurate measurements, scientists estimated the object to be an asteroid, mostly stone, weighing 100 to 1,000 tons. Its diameter was between 12 and 260 feet, somewhere between a school bus and a football field.

The flying rock skipped off the atmosphere, like a thrown stone skipping across the surface of a lake, and shot off into space. If the rock was the large size estimated and had approached at a steeper angle, it might have caused an explosion like the one over the Tunguska River in 1908.

By 1997, the stone will complete fourteen orbits of the sun and pass a point in space four days before Earth arrives at the same point. But these figures are only estimates. The stone could pass this "crossroads" in space as much as twelve days before or four days after Earth gets there. It's also possible that our planet and the stone will arrive at the same point in space at the same time and collide.

• On January 23, 1982, an asteroid a quarter mile wide passed 2.5 million miles from Earth. This near miss was the closest known flyby since 1976. In that year, a 600-foot asteroid—wide as two football fields joined end to end—zoomed by a mere 700,000 miles away.

• On May 5, 1986, Carolyn Shoemaker, using a telescope at Palomar Observatory in southern California, photographed a slow-moving asteroid. The object seemed to be going the wrong way, that is, against the direction of the main belt of asteroids.

After more photographs on the next few nights, she came to a frightening conclusion: The asteroid appeared slow because it was heading for earth; it was like viewing a rifle bullet head-on as it approached rather than seeing it speed by.

A radio telescope traced the asteroid and found it to be several miles wide and black as a piece of charcoal. Numbered 1986 JK, the object sped by earth on June 1 at a distance of 2.6 million miles, another close shave in astronomical terms.

But the near miss didn't end the story. After plotting the asteroid's orbit, Shoemaker determined that it will pass Earth every fourteen years—around Independence Day in the year 2000 will be its next flyby—if it doesn't collide with Mars or Jupiter first.

• The year 1989 seemed to be an exceptional one for fly-bys. Thirteen new Earth-crossers were discovered, five in one observation period in late October and early November.

In March, 1989 FC (later named 4581 Asclepius) passed within 450,000 miles of Earth—see page 10. (Asteroids are assigned identifying numbers by the Minor Planet Center. For 1989 FC, *1989* is the year of discovery. *F* is the sixth half month of the year—this asteroid was discovered on March 23. *C* means that it was the third asteroid discovered in that period. The discoverer selects a permanent name which must be approved by the International Astronomical Union.)

In June, a two-mile-wide asteroid passed Earth at a distance of 8 million miles.

Two months later, on August 9, one of the most unusual Earth-crossing asteroids yet seen was discovered by astronomer Eleanor Helin using the forty-eight inch Schmidt telescope at Palomar Observatory.

Helin spotted the asteroid, later named Castalia, as a streak of light on a photograph. It was still far away, but on a course that would bring it close to Earth. She alerted another astronomer, Steven Ostro, and gave him orbital data on the asteroid's course.

In Puerto Rico on August 22, Ostro headed a team that focused the 1,000-foot-wide radio telescope at Arecibo Observatory on the approaching asteroid. The huge dish sent out radar waves that produced an electronic image of the object, its distance and course, and revealed a surprise: Castalia turned out to be two asteroids held together by their weak gravity. The image showed a dumbbell-shaped object that rotated like a propeller every four hours.

Calculations of Castalia's flight showed that it traveled from the asteroid belt to the zone between Venus and Mercury every 400 days on its path around the sun. The asteroid passed Earth at a distance of 2.1 million miles. It will not come within several million miles of Earth again for another fifty years.

Of the numerous Earth-crossers discovered that year, Helin said, "If we are finding two or three asteroids a year this close to Earth, there is strong evidence of a sizable population of these objects that can cause great devastation. It's the one we don't see that's going to surprise us."

Smaller asteroids also travel in Earth-crossing orbits. A University of Arizona astronomer estimated 300,000 at least 300 feet across. But in the night sky, these rocks are hard to detect.

At 10:25 p.m. on January 18, 1991, at Arizona's Kitt Peak, a faint streak appeared on a computer image of the night sky. A small asteroid, thirty-three feet in diameter, was approaching Earth at 20,000 miles per hour.

Twelve frightening hours later, astronomers sighed with relief. The speeding rock was missing Earth by 102,300 miles, less than half the distance to the moon. Had Earth's gravity reeled it in, the rock would have struck with the destructive force of the atom bomb that had leveled Hiroshima, Japan, in World War II.

Another close call came on July 4, 1994, when 1994 NE, nearly 1,600 feet wide, passed a mere 1.6 million miles from our planet.

Astronomers who observe the night skies each month say the threat of a collision between Earth and a rogue asteroid is very real. On average, asteroids or comets fifty to one hundred feet wide or so strike earth every 200 to 300 years. Collisions with larger asteroids a third of a mile wide occur only once in 10,000 years.

Still, the asteroid with Earth's name on it is out there. Of this astronomers who deal with inner space are convinced.

"The earth is bound to be hit again sometime," said Clark Chapman, astronomer at the Planetary Science Institute in Tucson, Arizona. "It's unlikely that a really large asteroid will hit in our lifetime, but it's not beyond possibility. The earth is like a target in space."

"The danger is real—if we don't do something, human society could be wiped out," said Tom Gehrels, astronomer at the University of Arizona. "That thing may be out there right now."

# The Incoming Asteroid 12

At 12:26 p.m. on June 19, 1968, the asteroid Icarus, which is nearly a mile in diameter, will crash into the mid-Atlantic Ocean 2,000 miles east of Florida.

"Its impact—the same as a 500,000-megaton bomb blast—will splash out some 1,000 cubic miles of seawater and form a crater 15 miles across in the ocean floor. Tidal waves 100 feet high will sweep across coastal cities on both sides of the ocean. Earthquakes 100 times worse than any ever recorded will be felt all over the world.

"Clearly, Icarus must be stopped. No expense will be spared, and the only limitation is time. The program to stop Icarus must succeed."

This chilling and desperate problem was presented in 1967 to a class of twenty-one student engineers at the Massachusetts Institute of Technology in Cambridge. Working together, the students had to come up with a way to prevent the asteroid from colliding with earth and causing worldwide destruction.

The problem of the incoming asteroid was not real. It was a classroom exercise to test the students' skills and knowledge.

But the asteroid itself was very real. Sometime in the past, Icarus had escaped from the asteroid belt and now followed an odd orbit. In its journey through the solar system, it came to within 17 million miles of the sun, closer than any other asteroid, then shot 183 million miles away—some 40 million miles beyond Mars—before returning for another pass around the sun.

In its flight, Icarus passes close to Earth's orbit every thirteen months. Every fourteen years, however, it comes uncomfortably close to our planet, a mere 4 million miles in 1968.

The close flyby in 1968 gave the professor at MIT the idea for the problem: Let's say Icarus won't pass Earth safely this time, he told the students. Let's say it's going to hit Earth. What can you do to prevent such a disaster?

For fifteen weeks, the students discussed the problem. They talked with astronomers and other space scientists. They huddled in study groups. Then they were ready to present their solution to the problem.

To prevent Icarus from crashing into Earth, they decided to use six Saturn 5 rockets. Each rocket would be tipped with a powerful nuclear bomb.

Their plan called for the first rocket to be fired on April 7, 1968. Icarus would still be 100 million miles away, slightly farther than the sun. Radar would track the asteroid and steer the rocket with its warhead to a meeting point in space. (Radar is an instrument that can detect objects in space, like an airplane, by sending out radio signals. The signals bounce off the object and return to the radar. The instrument then determines the object's height, distance, and course.)

The students calculated that, on June 6, the rocket and Icarus would meet in space. Set off by a radio signal, the bomb would explode one hundred feet from the asteroid as it sped by. The powerful blast, they hoped, would nudge the speeding asteroid out of its path, and it would pass Earth at a safe distance.

If the first shot missed or failed to deflect Icarus, the students still had five shots left. Four of these bombs could be used to turn the asteroid or break it up into large pieces.

The sixth and last bomb would be saved until the final day. Heading into space in a last attempt to save Earth, the Saturn 5 would meet the incoming asteroid just 1.2 million miles away. Booming along at 65,000 miles per hour, Icarus would strike Earth in just eighteen hours.

Would the plan work? No one knows, of course. But the students' professor thought the plan was practical. "A 90 percent chance of success," he said.

Fortunately, the problem tested the skills of the twenty-one young engineers in the classroom only. But in real life, Icarus and other Earth-crossing asteroids pose an ongoing threat to our planet. Could a way be found, in our modern scientific age, to prevent large asteroids from striking earth?

In 1981, NASA—the National Aeronautics and Space Administration—brought a group of scientists together at Snowmass, Colorado, to discuss the problem. A NASA official explained the purpose of the meeting: "The risk of our planet being hit by a killer asteroid someday is very real, even though it may seem rather remote."

During the meeting, the scientists discussed many sides to the problem, the first of which was basic: how to spot an incoming asteroid among all the points of light in the night sky.

Viewed through a telescope, an object heading directly toward Earth appears not to move—like the light of a faraway train approaching on a track. An incoming asteroid might look like another star. Only at the last moment would it appear to move very fast, and by that time it would be too late to avoid the catastrophe about to happen. Once an asteroid entered Earth's atmosphere streaming fire, only seconds would pass before it struck.

Size was another problem. An asteroid a half mile wide could be detected 2.5 million miles away, more than ten times farther away than the moon. But the impact would be only five days away, barely enough time to fire off rockets if they were ready on the launchpad.

Another part of the problem was timing—early warning was essential. A scientist from the Jet Propulsion Laboratory in Pasadena, California, said, "Deflecting an incoming asteroid really depends on how much advance warning you have. The more warning, the less explosive power you need to nudge the asteroid from its path."

To deflect an asteroid three-quarters of a mile wide so

**LARGE ASTEROID HEADING FOR EARTH**

Early detection of a large asteroid on a collision course with Earth is necessary for an interception plan to work.

1. Astronomers calculate the day and hour when the paths of Earth and asteroid will meet in space and thus determine the positions of each.

2. A rocket tipped with a powerful nuclear device blasts off to intercept the incoming asteroid as far from Earth as possible.

3. The nuclear device explodes to one side of the asteroid to deflect it onto a new course away from Earth.

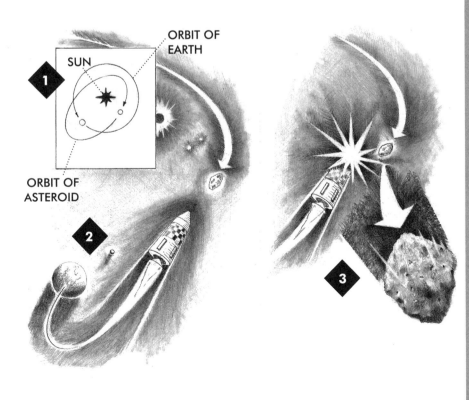

ORBIT OF EARTH

SUN

1

ORBIT OF ASTEROID

2

3

it would miss Earth by 6,000 miles—the minimum safe distance—a missile with a warhead as powerful as 14,000 tons of TNT would be needed, but only if the asteroid was still twenty days away from hitting Earth.

At a distance of only three days, a warhead as powerful as 580,000 tons of TNT would be required, a very large nuclear device.

The scientists thought that two places were best to set off an explosion: at aphelion and perihelion, the points in its orbit at which an asteroid is farthest from and nearest to the sun. At these points, only a small charge, as little as 200 pounds of TNT, might speed up or slow down an asteroid. A change in speed of only an inch per second would alter the asteroid's flight, thus causing it to pass by Earth at greater distances with each orbit.

But the scientists agreed that breaking up a large asteroid near Earth would not be practical. The broken fragments would still follow the same path as the parent asteroid and plummet to Earth.

"Consider being hit by a shotgun blast rather than a bullet," said Eleanor Helin. "Destruction is apt to be much more widespread. What we want to do is alter the asteroid's orbit just a little so the object won't hit Earth. Attaching a rocket or some other means of propulsion, such as a mass driver, is the general idea."

Asteroids the size of a bus or ocean liner, though, would continue to be a problem. These objects are detectable only when relatively close to Earth. They eventually could be detected earlier by satellites as they approach Earth and tracked from one to a few weeks before they were due to strike. Thus a warning of a collision might be possible.

The first step, then, to prevent a collision between

asteroids large or small and Earth, the scientists decided, was identification—locating those asteroids cruising through the solar system on Earth-crossing orbits. A large asteroid six miles wide could be spotted as far away as Jupiter. Its orbit could then be tracked on one of its flybys.

"We would need to observe an asteroid for five to ten years to know when it would hit," Tom Gehrels said.

The U.S. government now supports programs through the National Aeronautics and Space Administration to locate asteroids and comets in Earth-crossing orbits. In 1992, NASA sponsored the Near-Earth-Object Interception Workshop at Los Alamos, New Mexico, "to evaluate the threat to the Earth of asteroid and comet impacts and to explore remedial actions [to] prevent such disasters."

The scientists concluded that, at the present time, the only defense available against an incoming asteroid or comet would require a nuclear bomb to deflect the object. Within twenty years or so, however, other defenses could be developed, among them a device to pulverize a threatening space object; a "mass driver"—a kind of massive jet engine—attached to an asteroid to direct it on a new course; and solar sails—lightweight metal sails as large as two football fields that, pushed by the energy of the sun, would "sail" an asteroid away from Earth.

A project for the distant future might concentrate on a "billiard shot"—deflecting a small asteroid with a nuclear explosion into a larger asteroid and thus causing the larger asteroid to rebound on a new course.

But all plans, present and future, depend on early detection, the scientists warned, through "a comprehensive search for Earth-crossing asteroids and comets and a detailed analysis of their orbits."

Astronomer Eleanor Helin, wearing a warm coat to protect against the night cold, peers through the guide telescope of the eighteen-inch Palomar Schmidt camera telescope. With this telescope, she recorded 2062 Aten (white streak), nearly two miles in diameter, orbiting the sun but within Earth's orbit.
Eleanor Helin

Wide-angle telescopes like the eighteen-inch Schmidt camera photograph a broad patch of sky and record asteroids and comets moving against fixed—unmoving—stars. Using the Schmidt, observer Carolyn Shoemaker photographed 1986 EB for eight minutes against a backdrop of fixed stars. At Palomar Observatory, Helin and Shoemaker often discover three to four near-Earth asteroids in one month.
U.S. Geological Survey

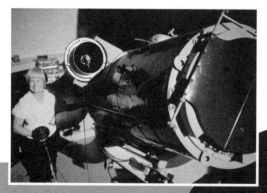

# 13 Asteroid Hunters

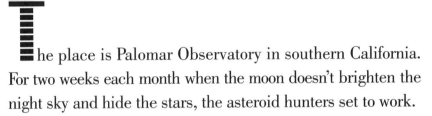

The place is Palomar Observatory in southern California. For two weeks each month when the moon doesn't brighten the night sky and hide the stars, the asteroid hunters set to work.

The observatory is the home of the famous Hale telescope. Although the Hale is the largest optical telescope in the U.S., it is not used to hunt asteroids. For this purpose, astronomers use two smaller ones, the eighteen-inch and forty-eight inch Schmidt telescopes.

Astronomers use the Hale to peer deep into space, toward the limits of the universe. Although it can see far, the Hale sees only a small section of the heavens, like looking through a keyhole at the night sky.

In contrast, the Schmidt telescopes see a large section of sky, an area about the size of the bowl of the Big Dipper. This broad view is necessary to record the flight of asteroids and comets across the points of light that are stars and far-off galaxies.

Nearly all near-earth asteroids discovered to date have

been found with Schmidt telescopes. Before 1973, asteroids were found in the course of general sky surveys or by accident on photographic plates of the night sky. In that year, however, the first deliberate search for near-Earth asteroids—the Palomar Planet-Crossing Asteroid Survey—was begun by Eleanor Helin and Eugene Shoemaker at Mount Palomar.

"The smallest [asteroid] that has been detected has a diameter somewhat larger than the length of a football field," says Helin. "We know objects of that size are out there, and we are concerned."

PCAS was the first near-Earth asteroid search program in any country. Along with Earth-crossing asteroids, the program has discovered seventeen active comets, asteroids that may be cores of dead comets, and more than 2,500 asteroids in the asteroid belt.

The program has also encouraged astronomers in other parts of the world to become involved in the search. Because of this worldwide effort, the discovery of near-Earth asteroids has more than doubled since 1979.

During the dark of the moon—the period just before the new moon—the asteroid hunters set to work. After the eighteen-inch Schmidt is aimed at a selected area of the night sky, film is inserted in the telescope and exposed for six minutes. Then the telescope is reset, new film inserted, and the same section of sky is photographed for a second time. The result is two photographs of the same area of the night sky.

After inserting the exposed films into a microscope with two eyepieces that show depth as well as height and width—three-dimensional images—the astronomer then compares the two films.

Each pair of films show roughly 10,000 points of light,

stars and distant galaxies. Light points that move —something that goes backward perhaps or across the film leaving a white streak—is an asteroid or comet. This patient, painstaking work rewards hunters with the discovery of about a dozen new Earth-crossing asteroids each year, although Helin found three during just one four-night period in the summer of 1990.

While astronomers at Palomar search the night skies, a few hundred miles to the east in Arizona, other astronomers search for Earth-crossers at Kitt Peak Spacewatch Observatory, one of more than a dozen observatories on Kitt Peak, a mountain 6,700 feet high near the border of Mexico.

Astronomers in the Spacewatch program use a special camera attached to a thirty-six-inch telescope. The camera doesn't use a film cartridge. Instead, an electronic instrument called a Charge-Coupled Device records what the telescope "sees" in the night sky and stores the information in a computer. The CCD is basically a TV camera or camcorder. It is far more sensitive to faint light in the night sky than is film. It converts light images, like stars, galaxies, and passing space objects, into electrical signals.

The Spacewatch telescope tracks across a section of sky for thirty minutes. Then the camera is turned off while the telescope is reset in its original position. The camera is then turned on and the track is repeated.

Astronomer Tom Gehrels stands by the thirty-six-inch Spacewatch telescope at Kitt Peak near Tucson, Arizona. Built in 1920, the telescope locates about two Earth-crossers per month plus another 2,000 rocks in the asteroid belt. The telescope is housed in a thirty-foot-high dome.
University of Arizona/Lori Stiles

The next step involves the computer. First, it matches the points of light recorded by each of the telescope's two tracks across the sky. Then it subtracts images on the first track from the second track by taking out fixed stars and galaxies—points of light that haven't moved—and keeps points of light that have moved, asteroids and comets.

A night's viewing might result in a hundred asteroids spotted in the asteroid belt, a few asteroids or comets close to earth, but no space object on a collision course.

In the early 1990s, the Spacewatch telescope at Kitt Peak located fifteen asteroids each year big enough "to eliminate human society," said Tom Gehrels, director of the program. Since then, that number has increased to as many as thirty-five asteroids in one year. By the mid-1990s, the number may reach one hundred.

Attaching CCDs to wide-view Schmidt telescopes, like those at Palomar, is the next step in the search for near-Earth asteroids. Existing Schmidt telescopes can be refitted with CCDs at one-tenth the cost of building a new telescope. A network of four instruments in the U.S. and other countries could, in twenty-five years, locate 90 percent of the 1,500 to 2,000 or so dangerous near-Earth asteroids so far uncharted, astronomers say.

Yet to be worked out: telescopes and electronic devices to spot asteroids as small as 150 feet, which, many astronomers warn, are a greater daily threat than the big rocks.

Discovering a small asteroid on a collision course with Earth, plotting its course, and evacuating people from the impact site might then reduce the chance of a disaster about to happen.

# 14 Outposts in Space

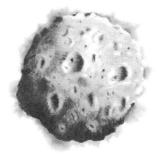

**P**rojects like Spacewatch and the Palomar Planet-Crossing Asteroid Survey are vital to locate asteroids on collision courses with Earth. But these investigations also serve another purpose: to gather information for what writers of history texts may someday call "the Great Exploration of the Solar System." In this grand adventure, asteroids will play an important role.

One purpose of space exploration is to find new sources of materials that are being mined out and used up on Earth.

A single asteroid wide as a football field and weighing a million tons could contain 200,000 tons of iron. It also could contain rich deposits of gold, platinum, and other precious metals worth millions of dollars.

A one- to two-mile-wide asteroid might hold high-grade nickel, iron, and magnesium with a value on Earth of 4 to 5 trillion dollars.

Space planners foresee cargo ships that could carry

## AN ASTEROID MINE IN SPACE

A mass driver—several miles long and powered by solar cells which convert sunlight into electricity—snares an asteroid wide as two football fields and weighing 1 million tons in a nylon net. Towing the asteroid past the moon (upper right), the space tug will "park" the asteroid in a high-altitude orbit above Earth. A factory erected on the asteroid will then mine its store of metals and build a space station.

Building structures from materials available in space is much less costly than hauling construction materials up from Earth against the tug of gravity. Precious metals like gold mined from the asteroid would be carried to Earth in large cargo ships.
NASA, Ames Research Center

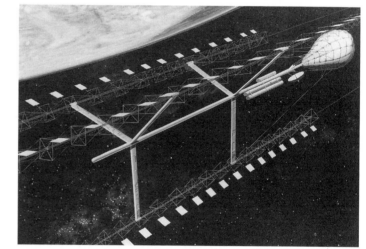

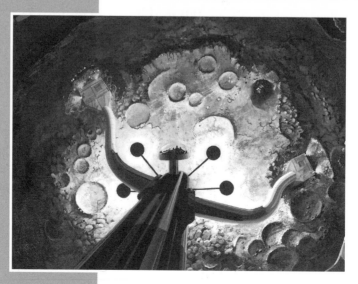

valuable ore to Earth for processing into useful metals. Another possibility: attaching a rocket engine to a distant asteroid, "driving" it toward Earth, and "parking" it in a nearby orbit so mining operations could begin.

Metals mined on asteroids and made into beams and girders in a space factory could also be used to build space colonies. This would save the enormous cost of transporting these materials from Earth. The moon is rich in silicon to make glass and bauxite to make aluminum. For a space-building program, asteroids could supply metals the moon lacks: iron, magnesium, and nickel.

For space explorers, an asteroid "filling station" in space would be invaluable. Some asteroids are made up of 20 percent water. About one-third of a spacecraft's weight is oxygen and hydrogen, fuel to propel the craft. These two gases could be extracted from an asteroid's water to refuel a spacecraft on its voyage into deep space, thus saving the weight of tanks and fuel during liftoff from Earth.

Another asset that asteroids offer space travelers is weak gravity. No need to expend fuel to "brake" for a soft landing. A spacecraft approaching a 1,500-foot-wide asteroid would take a half hour to "fall" the last 800 feet to its surface, touching down with the gentle impact of a pencil dropped from a half inch above a table.

Nor would the gravity of larger asteroids exert a much stronger pull. For a space craft to lift off an asteroid six miles wide would require a speed of only 9 miles per hour. In contrast, to escape Earth's gravity, rockets have to boost a spacecraft to 25,200 miles per hour.

From an asteroid, an astronaut could easily throw a baseball into deep space. Baseball pitchers on Earth hurl a ball at ninety miles per hour. Even at half this speed, the ball thrown from an asteroid would continue to travel after it passed out of sight.

About seventy-five near-Earth asteroids have been studied for possible missions. Seven or eight of these asteroids would be easier to land on than the moon, space planners say.

One project to explore asteroids is the Solar Sail spacecraft being developed by the World Space Foundation in California.

Solar Sail takes the clipper ship from the last century as its model. Fast-sailing clipper ships carried passengers and cargo to distant ports, propelled by the push of wind on their magnificent spread of sails.

"Sailing" spacecrafts use the same principle. Carried from earth into space by rockets, the Solar Sail unfurls a square metal sail the size of two football fields. Sunlight acts as a solar wind on the sail to push the craft. The solar wind is actually particles smaller than atoms blowing from the sun into space. These particles apply a light pressure on any object, like a metal sail, illuminated by the sun.

Besides visiting asteroids, a Solar Sail spacecraft with a sail 1¼th mile square could deliver supplies to space stations on distant asteroids and planets. Carrying the same load as the largest eighteen-wheel highway truck, a Solar Sail cargo craft could "sail" nearly 50 million miles from Earth to Mars in four years. Returning empty to Earth would require only two.

Close to Earth, a fleet of Solar Sails leaving for a journey into space would be visible to the naked eye. Those as far away as Mars could be seen through a small telescope.

Whether circling the sun endlessly in the asteroid belt or zipping by Earth, asteroids are very much in the future of people who inhabit our planet.

The possibility of a sizable asteroid slamming into earth and destroying civilization, while slim, is all too real. The craters of past impacts and the "loose cannonballs" of today crossing Earth's orbit provide a warning that astronomers take seriously.

Considering the consequences of such a catastrophe, we would be wise to follow two courses:

- Continue searching for likely Earth-crossers.
- Develop ways to avoid the coming collision in space that is bound to happen, if not tomorrow or next week, then surely some time in the future.

Preventing this doomsday impact from happening may be the single most important accomplishment in humankind's history.

# Your Own Space Rock

**Fragments of fallen asteroids lie
scattered about the Earth. Finding
one means knowing what to look for.**

In July 1966, astronaut Michael Collins, orbiting earth in
*Gemini 10*, saw a sight few humans have ever witnessed.
At a height of 475 miles (at the time a new high-altitude
record) the spacecraft was passing from day into night.
Collins could see lightning strokes along a line of thunder-
storms—and then an unforgettable spectacle: thin, fiery
trails of meteors streaking in from space, plunging into the
night, suddenly winking out.

High above Earth's atmosphere, Collins looked *down*
on the fleeting meteors. Watchers on the ground, however,
must look *up* to see the nightly display of meteors in their
final, flaming plunge to the planet.

What sky watchers see are mostly particles of space
rocks, sand grain size and larger, glowing from the friction
of the atmosphere fifty to eighty miles up, often six to ten
an hour—although a full moon or the glow of city lights
may obscure the trails.

While meteors the size of sand grains burn into dust-like ash, larger ones hit the ground, charred black from their swift passage through the atmosphere.

The charring is a natural process. In the twenty or so seconds that a meteor takes to pass through the air blanket around earth, the rock glows white-hot. But so swift is its passage that the heat can't sink in quickly enough to alter the interior of the rock. It's like holding an ice cube on a hot frying pan for a few seconds, then yanking it off. The surface has melted, but the interior is still ice.

While the surface of a meteor fuses to form a black, melted crust, the interior of the rock remains unchanged from the "cold soaking" it received in space for a few billion years.

How many meteorites survive a fall to Earth each year?

It's impossible to count the number, of course, but Glenn Huss, former director of the American Meteorite Laboratory, Denver, Colorado, estimated 200,000. "But," he added, "since about 70 percent of earth's surface is covered by water, only about 60,000 meteorites fall on dry land."

This figure suggests that meteorites lie scattered like pebbles on a beach just waiting to be picked up. Not the case.

Sixty thousand meteorites falling on Earth's 57.5 million square miles of dry land averages out to one meteorite per 1,000 square miles each year—about the area of Rhode Island.

In a state like Minnesota in the center of the North American continent—79,289 square miles of dry land (lakes and rivers bring the total to 84,402 square miles)—this meteorite fall amounts to about eighty meteorites per year.

As years pass, however, the number on the ground increases significantly. Since George Washington became president in 1789, perhaps 16,000 to 17,000 meteorites may have landed within Minnesota's boundaries. And the land goes back for eons before our first president took office.

Despite the number of meteorites that survive the fall to earth, space stones are difficult to find on the ground. One reason is their small size. Most stones that survive the fiery passage to earth measure a half inch or less and weigh perhaps ten grams or one-third of an ounce. Then again, the weathering of wind, rain, ice, and snow over years wears away at a stone and it disappears.

Still, meteorites do fall everywhere and large specimens can be found. Most are found accidentally, by farmers, ranchers, campers, and hikers who suddenly see an unusual rock on the ground and recognize a meteorite.

The best place to find meteorites?

Antarctica, the region around the South Pole. There, scientists venturing from their work stations easily spot the dark rocks on the pale blue ice.

As a source of meteorites, Antarctica offers another advantage. As wind blows off snow and then scours away the underlying ice, meteorites that fell ages ago become exposed. On the surface, they withstand weathering better than stones in northern climates. Thus more meteorites can be found in a single square mile in Antarctica than in other regions of the world.

In 1969, scientists in Antarctica found a scattering of five- to ten-inch specimens weighing ten to twenty pounds. Again in 1987–1988, twenty to twenty-five meteorites were recovered in an area searched only four years earlier with no findings.

In both instances, the stones had been frozen in the ice for years, maybe even hundreds or thousands of years. One of the largest meteorites recovered in Antarctica was a two-foot, 240-pounder now residing at the NASA-Johnson Space Center, Texas.

Second to Antarctica's ice sheet, deserts, plains, or areas of sparse vegetation offer the best chance of spotting a fallen space stone. A large number of meteorites are now being found in the deserts of Algiers in Africa and in Australia. The dry desert climate helps to preserve the stones.

A highly successful meteorite hunter was a professor at McPherson College in Kansas. Harvey Nininger's interest in meteorites began in 1923 when he witnessed a spectacular fireball in the sky. Before his death at age ninety-nine in 1986, Nininger wrote several books and 160 scientific papers on the subject. Arizona State University in Tempe now holds his collection of 6,000 meteorites.

Over the years, Nininger developed a special technique for finding these space rocks. He advertised in small-town newspapers, mostly in the midwestern U.S. His ads offered payment for them. He also called at

Meteorite-hunting geologists found this specimen on an ice field in Antarctica. The instrument being held above the rock is both a counter and a scale. Each meteorite found is given a number to identify it—the upper row of numbers. The number is imprinted on a metal tag that stays with the rock when it is shipped to the Johnson Space Center, Houston, Texas. There it is given a different, permanent number for study and storage. The second row of numbers is a scale, in centimeters, to approximate the size of the specimen.
NASA, Johnson Space Center

farms and asked about peculiar rocks farmers might have noticed in their fields.

In schools, he talked to students about meteorites. Always he brought along samples to show the kinds of stones he was looking for. His efforts were often rewarded when someone told about "a strange rock in the backyard." And when people learned that a neighbor had discovered a meteorite and had sold it for scientific research, more "strange rocks" suddenly turned up.

Nininger always asked a landowner's permission to search for meteorites, and he paid for those he wanted for his collection.

## FOUND: 6,000 METEORITES

A professor at McPherson College in Kansas, Harvey Nininger was a dedicated meteorite hunter. In 1939, Nininger (kneeling) took this magnetic rake—a trailer equipped with electromagnets—and, with son Robert, searched the area around Meteor Crater, Arizona, for fragments of the asteroid that had struck 50,000 years earlier.

Another device he used to locate buried meteorites, usually in farmers' fields, was a metal detector. One of some 6,000 meteorites he recovered was a black-crusted seventeen-pound stone near Hardwick in the southwestern corner of Minnesota.
American Meteorite Laboratory (3)

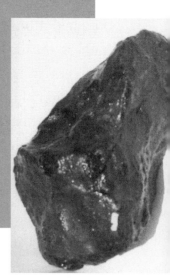

Today, the same guidelines exist. Nearly all sites of meteorite falls are on private land or on land owned by county, state, or federal governments. Before a meteorite specimen can be removed from public or private land, the law requires the consent of the landowner.

Meteor Crater in Arizona and land around the crater are examples of where meteorite fragments have been found. The crater is privately owned and the land around it belongs both to private owners and to the state. Any meteorite found in these places belongs to the owner of the land parcel on which it is found.

So if you find a rock that you think is a meteorite, first get permission of the landowner before you take it home.

Three types of meteorites survive the fall through Earth's atmosphere:

- **Stones.** The most common meteorites, stones account for about ninety-five of every one hundred space rocks found. Stony meteorites are rich in the same materials, but in different proportions, that make up almost all rocks on the earth's surface.
- **Irons.** Three or four of every one hundred meteorites are irons, which are made up almost entirely of nickel and iron.
- **Stony-irons.** Half rock and half metal. Uncommon. Only one or two of every one hundred meteorites are stony-irons.

How do you recognize a meteorite on the ground?

First, know what to look for. If at all possible, visit a natural history or science museum to view meteorites on display.

Most meteorites appear rusty brown from weathering—sun, rain, freezing, thawing. Prolonged weathering causes some meteorites to look like common field rocks and thus they are passed by.

A rare stony-iron was recovered from a grassy slope of a ranch near Albin, Wyoming, after the landowner attended a meteorite exhibit in Denver. The meteorite had gone unrecognized for twenty years.

All meteorites—even stony specimens—contain some iron. So a simple magnet is a good first test to determine if a rock is a meteorite.

Meteorites feel heavier than field rocks because of iron in their makeup. Irons are far heavier for their size than field rocks. If you ever did come upon a one-cubic-foot iron, you wouldn't be able to lift it; it would weigh 450 pounds. Metal detectors often locate irons buried in the ground.

Look for rounded edges on a rock. As the rock passes at high speed through earth's air blanket, friction causes melting, which smooths rough edges.

The passage also chars the rock, and creates a fusion crust—a thin, melted layer—that slowly cools. This black

A collection of stony meteorites found near Bruderheim, Alberta, Canada. A dark fusion crust and shallow surface pits identify many meteorites. Light surfaces show the interior of the meteorite. The stone may have broken apart in flight or upon striking earth. Geological Survey of Canada (GSC 112350)

crust appears only on freshly fallen, unweathered meteorites.

All meteorites, whatever the type, can be identified by holding them against an emery wheel or by scrubbing a rounded corner with emery cloth (backed by a 1-by-2-inch block of wood for support). Emery is a fine abrasive used to grind and polish metal or wood. Emery cloth is available at hardware stores.

- Stony meteorites show bright flecks of nickel-iron in the polished area.
- Irons reveal a solid, bright, nickel-iron interior.
- Stony-irons display flecks of metal and olivine (olive green) crystals in the stony matrix (interior pattern or makeup) and sometimes sizable nuggets of solid nickel-iron.

Geologists warn about using a file to scrape a specimen—for good reason. A meteorite (and most earth rock) is harder than a file. Rasping a file against a suspected meteorite grinds bits of the file's metal teeth into the rock. The specimen then appears to be saturated with metal when it really may not be.

If there is a question about a specimen—meteorite or common field rock—the geology departments of many state universities will test a specimen without charge.

The American Meteorite Laboratory, P.O. Box 2098, Denver, CO 80201, is another source of free testing.

Send a small specimen whole to these testing locations. For larger specimens, use a hammer and break off a piece about the size of a walnut. Always say in a note where and when the stone was found. Enclose postage if you want the stone returned.

Some testing laboratories will offer to buy a stone if it turns out to be a meteorite.

Mail-order firms provide meteorites for sale and offer catalogs at modest cost from which to select whole or cut specimens.

Photos in these catalogs show the colorfully patterned and veined interiors of many stones and reveal what the interiors of the parent asteroids must have looked like as they slowly formed in the gas and dust of the infant solar system billions of years ago.

These mail-order companies often advertise in the space and want ad sections of science and natural history magazines available in many libraries.

# More Reading on Asteroids

## BOOKS

Books on space science in your school or public library offer much good reading on asteroids. Check the index under "Asteroids" to see what a book might present.

Some special titles on this subject include:

Burrows, William E. *Exploring Space: Voyages in the Solar System and Beyond.* New York: Random House, 1990.

Chapman, Clark R., and David Morrison. *Cosmic Catastrophes.* New York and London: Plenum Press, 1989.

Frazier, Kendrick, and the Editors of Time-Life Books. *Solar System.* Alexandria, Va.: Time-Life Books, 1985.

Gallant, Roy A. *National Geographic Picture Atlas of Our Universe.* Washington, D.C.: National Geographic Society, 1986.

Hartmann, William K., and Ron Miller. *The History of the Earth: an Illustrated Chronicle of an Evolving Planet.* New York: Workman Publishing Company, 1991.

Jastrow, Robert. *Journey to the Stars: Space Exploration—Tomorrow and Beyond.* New York: Bantam Books, 1989.

Sagan, Carl, and Ann Druyan. *Comet.* New York: Random House, 1985.

WGBH Boston. *Nova: Adventures in Science.* Reading, Mass. Addison-Wesley, 1982.

## PERIODICALS

Asteroids is a subject that is constantly evolving as astronomers and earth scientists continue to make discoveries about these space objects. Magazines that provide ongoing information are:

*Ad Astra* (monthly)
*Astronomy* (monthly)
*Aviation Week & Space Technology* (weekly)
*Minor Planet Observer* (monthly)
*Science* (weekly)
*Science News* (weekly)
*Sky and Telescope* (monthly)

To find articles on asteroids appearing in these magazines and in nearly all magazines published in the U.S. and Canada, try these two indexes:

*Readers' Guide to Periodical Literature*
*Magazine Index*

Available in most public libraries, they list titles of articles on asteroids (and thousands of other subjects) and give names and dates of magazines in which the articles appear. Subjects are arranged alphabetically. Start with "Asteroids." This may lead you to "Cosmology," "Space Flights," "Telescopes," "Universe," and more.

Books and magazines not available in the collection of a library may often be borrowed from other libraries. Librarians can assist with interlibrary loans.

# Index